# The Winter Garden and Other Stories

Hayden Thorne

Published by Hayden Thorne, 2019.

# Also by Hayden Thorne

**Arcana Europa**
Guardian Angel
The Flowers of St. Aloysius
Hell-Knights
Children of Hyacinth
The Amaranth Maze
A Murder of Crows

**Curiosities**
Dollhouse
Automata
Eidolon

**Dolores**
Ambrose
Echoes in the Glass
A Dirge for St. Monica

**Ghosts and Tea**
The Ghosts of St. Grimald Priory
Agnes of Haywood Hall

A Most Unearthly Rival
The Haunted Inkwell
The House of Creeping Dolls


**Grotesqueries**
A Castle for Rowena
The Rusted Lily
Primavera


**Masks**
Masks: The Original Trilogy
Curse of Arachnaman
Mimi Attacks!
Dr. Morbid's Castle of Blood
The Porcelain Carnival


**Standalone**
Renfred's Masquerade
Rose and Spindle
Gold in the Clouds
Helleville
Icarus in Flight
Arabesque
Banshee
Wollstone
The Glass Minstrel
Henning
The Twilight Gods
The Book of Lost Princes
The Winter Garden and Other Stories

Desmond and Garrick
The Cecilian Blue-Collar Chronicles


Watch for more at https://haydenthorne.com.

# Table of Contents

# The Haunted Glade

It was a haunted glade; no one was welcome. Local tongues wagged, and twilight tales were spun within decrepit cottages and throughout the bleak countryside. Intricately woven tapestries of sinister origins turned into tradition. A man who practiced the black arts was exiled there by a long-forgotten saint. A man who had mortgaged his soul for the sake of his beloved met his end there, but as to how, no one really knew. A demon was born to the village whore, and there he was abandoned by his mother, who promptly vanished with not much left to her name but a clump of torn and bloody hair on her bed of filth.

Weathered faces leered behind the shadows of the hearth, toothless mouths working busily to fill the bleak evenings with newer, more outlandish versions of ancient legends. Youthful faces stared back, enthralled, those humble fireside lessons slowly woven within impressionable minds. Children paid terrified heed to their elders. Adolescents listened and secretly swore to prove these tales a falsehood. Young adults, on the cusp of greater responsibilities, catalogued them for future use should their own children dare to step beyond the line. They received some much-needed support from the village potter.

"Legends wouldn't be what they are today had they not any basis in truth," Irwin Blythe said as he loaded his cart with his pottery in preparation for his weekly trip to the market.

"And what truth would this be?" some of the boys demanded in exasperation. "We've heard so many stories about the glade!"

"I've heard so many, myself, which only convinces me that something real holds them all together; otherwise, they wouldn't sound almost alike, would they?"

The girls sulked and restlessly tugged at their shawls or aprons. "That doesn't sound very convincing at all."

"Sometimes we've got nothing to go by but blind faith."

Around him a small group of awestruck children and skeptical adolescents gathered to see him off. He'd always been a great favorite of the locals, having won them over with his good nature, irrepressible humor, humility, and wealth of stories, the last point being regarded everywhere as a rare gift, for none of his stories fell along ordinary lines. His tales, no matter what the length, were all intricately plotted and full of fantastical foreign elements. A good number of people were convinced that elves or fairies whispered them in his ear as he lay sleeping at night. And Irwin Blythe would have suffered the indignity of superstitious gossip had he not been shielded by collective pity.

The potter, after all, was thirty-six, and he'd never married—nor did it seem as though any woman was keen to cast her net on him anytime soon or, indeed, ever. He courted a couple in his younger years, but he was thwarted, and he'd given up in spite of people's encouragement. Oddly enough, women were repelled by him though when asked, none could think of a convincing answer to their immediate and strong refusal to attract his attention. He was tall and shaped by years of hard labor, his complexion browned by the sun, his hair always powdered with dry clay or dust from the road. He bore scars from his work, but he wasn't a disagreeable-looking fellow by any means; in fact, the children liked the way he smiled, for when he did, the vibrant hazel of his eyes always vanished into cheerful slits edged with creases.

"I see no reason why anyone should fret over me," Irwin laughed. "I'm quite happy living alone, really, and I've got my work to consider. Besides, I travel far too often for me to be a more proper husband and father."

And it was true. Sometimes Irwin Blythe would vanish from the village and not return for seven days straight. He'd look thoroughly exhausted when he came home, but he was pleased and, on the whole, rejuvenated. Moreover, he'd have new stories to share with the children of the village, who were always excited to see him return from his travels.

"Ah, you poor dear," some of the older women sighed. "It's such a waste of youth and character not to have your good qualities passed down to your children."

"Oh, come, Grandmama," adolescent boys and girls laughed. "Nothing happens without a reason, and we're convinced that Master Blythe is serving a very important purpose being the way he is."

"And what would that be, pray?"

"It's not for anyone to know, of course! Some things are never meant to be discovered!"

Some elders scoffed, and some smiled indulgently. "You make him out to be like some kind of supernatural creature."

"Maybe he is," a few of the girls said with energy. They seemed to believe it, or perhaps they wished to.

The youngsters would find so much amusement in the thought, having out-witted their superiors again by dipping into Irwin's own words for their purpose, while their older counterparts shook their heads. There was no arguing against the young, they knew, and it was *sometimes* best to let them discover their own mistakes as they grew, for that was how wisdom would be nurtured.

And so in time, the perpetual bachelor was left alone; Irwin was welcomed by everyone to their supper tables, and in his neighbors he found his family. His unusual and unsettling stories kept the younger children from venturing into the wood, where the haunted glade lay hidden. For his part, that was all he needed, and he secretly exulted over his success with them. He had more trouble, however, with the older ones.

Among the restless youth, attempts at disproving legend served to muddy things. A new rumor began to be whispered among them about faint music wafting through the trees—a siren's call from the haunted glade. They listened, straining, at various times of the day, with some standing in rapt attention beyond the edge of the wood, some stretched out on the grass with their ears pressed against the earth, some embracing the ancient trees that marked the wood's borders. They braved the winds and the rain, and some even dared to defy the snow, at times with tragic consequences.

Three youngsters, all of whom had grown up very close as friends, had braved the harsh weather on three separate occasions. Two had fallen desperately ill after losing their way in the trees and being exposed to the elements for too long, and they never recovered. The third, undeterred by his friends' conditions, took it on himself to search for the haunted glade at night, and he never returned. A frantic search the following day yielded nothing, and his body wasn't discovered till four days after his disappearance. As it was with his friends, he'd lost his way.

A shocked village buried the dead and mourned. Irate and terrified parents demanded that their children steer clear of the wood, with threats of severe punishment hanging over the youngsters' heads. Boys and girls listened, shaken and cowed, and as time passed and blunted the horror and grief of their friends' deaths, they began to exchange whispers about strange music again. One by one, they crept out and inched their way closer to the wood's borders, straining their ears.

"I heard no music," was the disappointed conclusion, and the elders' weathered faces scoffed before the hearth, admonishing them with the added claim that only damned souls were meant to hear it.

"Who said there's music?" they asked each other in hoarse whispers as they gathered together, far, far away from the rest of the village by the edge of a pond that many believed to be the real entrance to the haunted glade.

They were a circle of girls and boys in the flowering of youth. Every so often someone would catch another's eye as though he or she had just been seen for the first time by a potential admirer. And little by little, in spite of the gravity of their exchange, young minds bloomed under each other's influence.

"I don't know. I heard it from Phineas."

"Really? I thought it was Cordelia."

"No, it must have been Guendolen or Luther."

"Well, whoever started it has a lot to answer for now. Jack, Godfrey, and Oleda are dead and gone..."

"It's no one's fault but theirs," came the rushed and emphatic defense from all around. "No one told them to do something as stupid as to wander off in the rain or snow to look for the music! Godfrey went out in the dead of night, too, and look where he is now."

Arguments, accusations, and all sorts of puzzled and guilt-ridden remarks wove their way through the group, but none was ever answered or proven to their satisfaction. The deaths of friends had left an undeniable mark on the youngsters, and they were forced to concede that their zealous, thoughtless energy had contributed to the tragedies; no one could accuse anyone specifically for starting the rumor, but they all understood how they'd influenced each other into attempting things that crossed all bounds of reason.

They all agreed not to speak of it for a while—at least until the village had recovered further from its shock and had moved on.

Irwin Blythe was bothered by the turn of events. He'd heard the whispered exchanges about strange music, and he'd been on his guard since then, for he knew what it all meant. He watched—as closely as he could without rousing anyone's suspicion—the anxious group of adolescents, more specifically the boys, for any sign that would confirm the thought that now gnawed through his mind day and night. By and large they seemed to be going about their business quite normally in spite of their discomfort.

One by one, he caught the way wordless signals were exchanged between boy and girl, the way distance shrank between them and conversation took on a newer, more self-conscious tone, and they began to behave as though they were meeting strangers for the first time. Then they walked off in pairs, young heads bent close to each other in confidential exchanges. Irwin watched adolescent romance take shape among them—all except one.

Yves Milford was the butcher's son, and he was lost in an attitude of admiration whenever he was in the company of a certain youngster his age. He smiled readily, he blushed, shrugged a great deal, looked at the ground, kicked a pebble or two, met his adored one's gaze with a shy, fearful look of hope. But it was a fruitless situation for him, Irwin knew too well, for Yves's blossoming infatuation was fixed on another boy. He was a good friend of Yves who'd always treated him well, but he was impervious to Yves's quiet courtship, having already won the affection of a rosy-cheeked dairy maid. And heaven only knew what he'd do to Yves if he were to discover his friend's misplaced love.

"Ah, the poor lad," Irwin murmured, watching Yves's smile fade as he stepped away from the scene, leaving his friend free to walk off with his girl on his arm.

The potter's heart sank; he now knew the answer to the riddle. Yves must have let slip, however innocently, word about the mysterious music that filtered through the trees around the haunted glade. He was the only one in his group who could hear it—aside from Irwin. There was no doubt now, given what the boy had in common with the potter.

Irwin knew what was to come. Yves had been noticed and was now marked by legend, and the potter could do nothing about it other than to offer comfort to the boy should Yves require it. In fact, he expected Yves to seek out kindred spirits if only for the purpose of companionship and solace, just as Irwin did several years ago, when he was Yves's age.

In the meantime, however, there was the matter of boundless curiosity to consider. Time had passed, grief over lost friends faded, and spring was soon there, stirring imagination and energy like never before. The wood and its haunted glade were eyed with fiercer interest.

. . . .

PERHAPS, YOUTHFUL ADVENTURERS declared, one ought to simply venture forth and search, music or no. And so they tried, carving new paths through the wood, which led them nowhere. Serpentine trails meandered and fooled hopeful spirits with the promise of adventure. The ageless trees themselves seemed to aid them. Gnarled roots quietly pushed their way through the earth, stretching their reach, marking the limits of a given trail with their bumpy outlines. Branches shifted and bent down, blocking one's view past a given tree, their leaves thickening and spreading themselves out into a black-green curtain. If one persisted in pushing past these obstacles, fingerlike twigs would claw at tender flesh, or snakelike roots would curl around an ankle, and the adventurer, chastised, had no choice but to turn around.

"It's hopeless!" a girl cried as she sat on the grass with her friends, rubbing her scraped ankles.

"The way the paths seemed to change, one would think that the wood's under a spell," another said while impatiently lacing her weathered boots. One of her heels had caught against a root as she wandered through the trees, and her struggles to free herself had nearly torn the boot apart.

"Perhaps it is. Didn't they say that the glade's haunted by a he-witch?"

"A sorcerer!"

"No, a demon!"

Their voices rose to fill the clear, spring afternoon air as boys and girls argued, confounded by the manifestation that had thrown such a deep and lasting shadow over their beloved woodland. They all hobbled home, exasperated and wounded, to be met with the sight of aging family members shaking their heads as they crossed the threshold of their respective cottages.

These white-haired and weathered faces smiled indulgently in their triumph, toothless mouths hard at work in pressing the matter of a forbidden glade. "Didn't we tell you so?" they crowed again and again.

Yves Milford sat quietly in his chair and listened to his share of scolding from his parents without a word of protest. He ate obediently what meager supper was prepared for him; he went about helping his mother clean the soiled dishes and sweep the cracked stone floor before retiring for the night. Earlier that day, the boy had tried to romance a childhood friend—an apple-cheeked girl who once declared that she'd marry him if he asked. Only now, she demurred without a reason, offering him nothing more than smiles of pity and regret when she rejected his suit. As Yves curled up under his patched-up blanket and stared into the darkness, his mind struggled to find something meaningful in the puzzles that continued to dog his steps since he turned sixteen almost two years ago.

He wondered why he was the only one who could hear the music of the trees in the twilight hours. He couldn't understand why he found strange new paths that seemed to lure him deeper into the wood whenever he was alone in his exploration, and yet these same paths would vanish when he was in the company of another person. He never tried to venture into the waiting shadows that called out to him, but whenever he heard the strange music in the waning hours, something assured him that his time would come soon enough. He wondered why he was in love with a boy. He wondered why he couldn't get a girl to love him, for he was convinced that a woman's affection would be the cure to his strange propensities.

He passed a thin hand across his brows as he blinked, blue eyes fixed in the direction of the wood when he murmured, "Just like Master Blythe."

His spirits rose at the thought of a fellow oddity. That Irwin was well liked among the locals added a strong sense of comfort to the sudden connection he found. Perhaps, Yves thought, perhaps someday he'd be enjoying the same collective affection that the potter now enjoyed, especially if he were to remain hopeless in his search for companionship.

A tentative little smile broke across Yves's pale young face, and he sank into a deep and fitful sleep after a whispered prayer of thanks. He also reminded himself to nurture his friendship with Irwin Blythe, whom he now considered, in a rush of naïve hope, his best friend. He was sure that his parents wouldn't object to inviting the potter to his eighteenth birthday supper, which was a week away.

Yves sought out Irwin's company. It proved to be a more difficult thing than expected since the potter kept odd hours, and Yves himself helped his father, often working long and hard days that left him with nothing else but enough time to stumble home. All the same, he made sure to strike a friendly conversation at every opportunity, which Irwin seemed to accept without question. The older man also encouraged it, a wistful smile lighting his sunburnt features as he conversed with the boy. Yves took no trouble at all in hiding his appreciation of a fellow misfit's company, and he was always lively and relieved whenever they were together. He retired for the night feeling more confident about himself, and he never forgot to pray his thanks for Irwin's presence in his life.

Three days before Yves's eighteenth birthday, the two friends were walking past the wood on their way home from the market. Irwin was entertaining his young companion with new stories that enthralled the boy, who could barely walk straight and listen at the same time, his attention being so rapt.

Irwin suddenly paused in his tracks. "There," he breathed. His gaze, though fixed ahead of him, had softened as though he were lost in a sudden daydream. "Do you hear it?"

Yves fell silent and listened. From somewhere in the wood, past the thick wall of ageless trees, a light, cheerful tune could be heard. It drifted lazily along with the breeze, sweet and melodic and pensive at the same time. The boy glanced at Irwin and watched him for a few seconds in thoughtful silence. Then he nodded.

"I do," he said quietly.

Irwin returned his gaze, and to Yves, the potter seemed to have been transformed by the twilight music, his dark, scarred, and tired features softening into youth and renewal. "It's not frightening," he said with a beatific smile. "It might be at first, but it never is. No harm's ever meant. The only harm, really, was his being forced into an eternity of this."

"By whom?"

"Those who claimed to do good by us all. They saw what he was, and they drove him away, cursing him with prayers for his damnation."

Yves understood well enough. "He's like us, you mean."

"Like us, yes."

The boy looked at the clustered trees. "You see him then. I suppose those days when you leave us, you go to him."

Irwin's smiled deepened. "And I'll go to him for the last time soon, young Yves."

"I won't see you again?"

"You will, and you won't. But don't worry, lad. Someday you'll follow my steps, and you'll find me at the end of the road—along with the others. There've been several of us through the years, you know. Never think that you're alone."

Irwin looked quite pleased at the prospect as though he'd been anticipating this journey for a long time now, and he was more than ready to take it on.

Yves frowned. "Is he a demon?"

Irwin laughed, his voice coarse and dry. "Hardly!" When he calmed down, he glanced at Yves, his smile soft and wistful. "To say that this is simply the way of things is wrong and an affront to those who came before you and especially to him. Think of it as protection. Solace. Liberation."

Yves could only stare back at Irwin and then sigh, scratching his head. "I don't understand you, but I'm guessing that I will someday."

"When it's time."

Little by little, though their conversation never stretched past this point, Yves thought that he could see where all this was going, and the puzzle pieces were slowly falling into place. He mulled over Irwin's own story of years of confusion and loneliness before the glade's music made itself heard. Now the potter's curious adventures neared their conclusion, and Yves mulled over his own newly forming path while they both walked home in silence.

On Yves's eighteenth birthday, Irwin Blythe left the village, never to return. His property remained untouched but was eventually seized by the crown; everything was sold off in bits and pieces.

"He told no one where he was going?" some of Yves' friends asked, and everyone exchanged confused and disappointed glances. "He left no note? No message at all?"

"I'm going to miss him and his stories. This dull old place won't be the same."

"I know. I wish I talked to him more." To this everyone agreed sadly. Irwin Blythe was a remarkable fellow and a popular man, but for all that, his eccentricities still served as a thin barrier separating him from the rest of the older villagers. Despite their ready welcome of him, there was still that curious distance of an arm's length that none of Yves' peers and younger children could understand.

"Well," Yves said after a mournful moment's pause. "Wherever he is right now, I'm sure he's quite happy." And he meant that. Irwin Blythe had bidden him a cheerful goodbye the previous day, apologizing for turning down Yves' invitation to his birthday supper.

"My dear boy," the potter had said, resting a thick, scarred, and heavy hand on Yves' shoulder. "You'll be eighteen tomorrow. It's your time now. I've another path to follow."

"Are you joining the others?"

"I am, and I look forward to it." Irwin Blythe grinned, and the marks of time and care showed themselves more deeply on his face. "You'll be well cared for, Yves Milford. Remember, you're not alone, and you never will be."

Yves nodded, smiling through his tears.

• • • •

AS TIME WENT, YVES'S friends gave up on childish play, having discovered a different brand of magic. They were soon young adults with thoughts of teaching their own children these cautionary tales, while a new generation of adventurers stepped forward. They met at times, laughing at their past reckless-ness and misguided bravery. None among their ranks, they declared with much confidence, had ever reached the legendary glade, much less seen its supernat-ural occupant. It was an ancient tale and nothing else—certainly a very effective warning against foolish attempts at wandering too far into the old wood, where salvation would be a lost cause. Courtships soon led to marriages, and the vil-lage was blessed with a new set of youthful faces, whose minds would soon be filled with local legend.

Among their ranks was the butcher's son, who had done his share of ad-venturing. Yves Milford laughed with his peers, scoffed along, raised a pint in a joking toast to adolescent frivolities, feigning carelessness. He shared his own fond recollections of lost friends.

He was now twenty-nine, and he was still a bachelor, which surprised everyone, for the boy had matured to a handsome man. Surely, was the puzzled consensus, female hearts ought to be drawn toward the sight of brown-gold hair and blue eyes, a quiet smile, and a figure shaped by years in honest labor, dress-ing animal flesh and dealing in meat? But women didn't think to flirt with him or encourage him in any way, offering no reason for their disinterest though they remained on friendly terms with him.

It almost seemed as though Yves Milford was protected by an unseen and possessive force that gently thwarted interest with a quiet, magic spell.

Yves had also developed a talent for storytelling, and he became a great favorite among the children, who sought him out for new, ever more fantastic tales that many believed were whispered in his ear by elves and fairies when he slept.

"Master Blythe taught him all he knows, I'm sure," some of the older folks said. "Remember how close they grew right before Master Blythe left?"

"Well, I suppose it's for the good of the children that someone's here to fill their heads with harmless nonsense—better that than to have them wander off into the wood and be lost to us."

Village elders' fading eyes stared at the brightly-lit hearths, and those who remembered the potter often asked the same questions as though they'd forgotten the answers. "What happened to Master Blythe? Has anyone heard anything of him yet?"

"I heard that he's now happily situated in the north."

"I heard that he set sail, though no one knows where he went."

There was no consensus, and Yves knew that there never would be one, but it hardly mattered to him. He merely glanced up at the sky and watched the birds, his gaze following a few, his heart comforted by the prospects that awaited him when his own time came.

And when his friends all scattered back to their cottages and in the waiting arms of their spouses and children, he walked back to his empty cottage to await the call. It came—as it had always done since he turned sixteen—a quiet, barely audible trill that heralded twilight, one for which he never needed to strain for him to hear. Then he threw on his coat and walked out, hurrying to the wood and through the trees that seemed to bow before him, moving back in reverence with their roots sinking into the earth and their branches lifting themselves high. He never needed light to find his way through the thick, oppressive growth. The music guided his steps and led him safely to the glade, where he'd stay for the next seven days, the way Irwin Blythe did before him.

• • • •

THE GLADE'S LONE OCCUPANT smiled in welcome, setting his flute aside before spreading his arms wide for an embrace. The man was ageless, for he'd lived there for centuries, bound to the glade into infinity though he was born mortal.

Yves paused at the clearing and observed him. What a cruel, inhuman thing, he thought bitterly, that this creature would be cursed for loving another man—chased out of the village with vindictive prayers heaped on his head for his eternal damnation by those who claimed to be arbiters of collective morality. Then his story would be distorted and hidden behind legends that reviled him for being a sorcerer, a demon, a monster whose soul had been mortgaged to the devil.

• • • •

YVES BRAVED THE MUSIC'S call after his eighteenth birthday several years ago. It was like a rebirth, he thought, as he made his first tentative journey to the glade. The emergence of the path leading to it. The woodland's silent displays of worship. The appearance of the glade's fairy-king, his gentle welcome to the amazed boy, his unhurried courtship of a young mortal who was, at heart, no different from him. Yves lost his innocence to his ageless lover soon after, and they spent many days lying on the grass, feeling renewed and watching the birds.

"Master Blythe is here, isn't he?" Yves asked one day, his tired gaze following a hummingbird as it flittered here and there, and he luxuriated in the feel of the fairy-king's robes beneath him, soothing his back with their rich texture and warmth.

"He's one of them, yes," the fairy-king replied and pointed at the birds.

"He's probably very pleased to be so free. Are there many up there who were like him—like us?"

"Many, but not all. Mortals and birds fly together."

Yves looked thoughtfully at their winged companions. "And they die together in the end."

"As all birds do in time." There was a moment's silence. "Do you think them to be cursed?"

"No, of course not. I'm sure Master Blythe—and all the others who loved you before—are happier now than they were. At least they're not as desolate as they used to be." Yves glanced at his companion and grinned. "I'll be up there, too, someday, guarding the glade, while you save another man from all that dreadful loneliness out there."

The fairy-king smiled back and raised himself on his elbows to kiss him. Cursed at the bloom of his youth, he was now forever fixed at twenty-one though the centuries had done their task in marking time on his person. He looked young and old, lively and tired, full of inexhaustible hope and burdened with unending sadness. His lovers through the years became his existence, with each young man following his predecessor once he turned eighteen. And the one before him graciously stepped aside and joined *his* predecessors when he walked through the path to the haunted glade that one final time. There would be the last kiss of gratitude and blessing from the fairy-king, and he'd stretch his arms to the sky, feathered limbs beating against the air as he flew off to freedom.

The fairy-king lavished them with stories, which they'd all taken back with them for the children's benefit. The village that had cursed him long ago now enjoyed his gifts.

· · · ·

THIS BEING THE SUMMER of Yves's twenty-ninth year, the leaves in the fairy-king's hair had now changed in hue—a little more faded than the spring. His eyes had also shifted from a deeper, more vibrant green to something softer, anticipating the gold and red of the coming autumn. His robes were no different, but it hardly mattered, for the butcher's son had always taken delight in their texture. Yves smiled when he crossed the leaf-strewn threshold toward the fairy-king.

A long finger touched his chest as he neared, and Yves' faded rags turned to water, trickling down his body in warm, soothing rivulets. As he lay on the grass within an embrace of leaves and bark and warmth that never faded, he wondered about his successor—a boy from a future generation meant to be marked by legend for no other reason than that he was what he was. What a revelation it would be to the fortunate youth, Yves thought as he pulled the fairy-king close, eagerly opening his mouth for a kiss. What a revelation, indeed, to discover freedom and not a curse, to enjoy the loving companionship which tradition denied him, and that loneliness was a thing of the past.

A young man, heavily cloaked in black wool, stood with head bowed by the marker. He'd placed a fresh bouquet of nosegays on the grave, taking care to arrange the flowers in what one would call "a studied wildness," which he'd always considered an appropriate description of his deceased beloved.

"The garden's growing very well," he said, his gaze resting on the name carved in marble, the graceful scrawl a pretty yet melancholy tribute to the occupant of the isolated grave. "The roses are climbing everywhere, and I've ordered the gardener to leave them alone. They want nothing more than to travel, and I, for one, won't stop them—won't limit their direction. I've taken down the rest of the shrubbery and left the grounds with nothing else but roses. Your favorite red and gold climbers are flourishing and have developed into beautiful, wild, sprawling shrubs."

He paused to smile lightly. "They're so much like you."

A sudden gust of cold wind blew, forcing him to pull the cloak more tightly around himself. He winced a little from the biting force against his skin then glanced up and found that the sun had disappeared behind a growing swirl of dark and gray clouds, the sound of dull thunder filling the otherwise quiet air around him. In the distance, he could barely see the Silesian Beskids, for much of the land in between his home and those glorious mountain ranges was already under the onslaught of a downpour.

"Again," he sighed, shaking his head before glancing back at the marker. "The sky never wants to see us together, does it?"

The name on the grave marker seemed to stare back at him. The young man smiled once more before kneeling down, tenderly brushing the cold marble for the hundredth time, and then pressing his lips against the stone.

"Till then," he murmured, resting his forehead against the stone and then standing up. "I'll be seeing you very soon."

With one final look, Konstancji turned and walked away, his head bent as his cloak flapped wildly in the wind, which had grown more and more insistent. He left the lonely grave that lay tucked away and protected in a small patch of land beyond his house's main grounds. It was situated by the edge of a dark, lifeless lake, a prime spot in the opinion of the still-grieving heir, one that protected his beloved from the unwanted presence of intruding visitors, be they friends or family.

Konstancji made his solitary way back to the desolate house, reluctant to abandon the grave and yet compelled to return and to resume the work he'd left.

He was almost done, thank the heavens. After a year—after so many willing sitters. He was finally catching a glimpse of the end of the road, and he'd soon rest and enjoy the fruits of his labor.

His eyes shone with a distant light at the notion, and his lips, grown cold and devoid of emotion since his loss, moved imperceptibly, not feeling the sting of yet another harsh gust of wind against his person.

"Just wait, Ziven," he whispered, his pace doubling. The first large drops of rain began to pelt him. "I've never forgotten about today."

An old woman—the only servant who lived with him—met him the moment he entered the rear door, curtsying and quietly receiving the cloak as he pulled it off his shoulders. She shuffled off without a word, disappearing around the corner of the dimly lit interior to carry on with her duties.

Konstancji walked off to the rear stairs—the ones that lay hidden from common use, accessible only through a narrow door that remained locked at all times. He fumbled for his keys, the metallic jangling sounds almost harsh to his ears as he searched for the right one among the five he'd linked together in one smallish ring, which he'd also attached to the end of his watch chain. He'd always thought that those keys, sharing space with a pocket watch, gave him a very accurate picture of the connection between time and locks. The resulting bulk was cumbersome—making it impossible for him to hide his pocket watch and forcing him to have a set of specially designed waistcoats with oversized pockets made. It was an inconvenience that he'd happily put up with for a year. After this day, Konstancji wouldn't have to carry those keys and pocket watch in such a manner anymore, and those waistcoats could be given away as cast-offs for his housekeeper's son.

The house being empty save for its two occupants, the silence that hung in the air was thick and heavy, adding to the oppressive atmosphere. What little sound there was thundered or screeched shrilly for a second or two before dying out in a muffled sigh against the weight of the stillness that lingered.

He didn't bother lighting a candle when he set foot on the bottom of the hidden stairs. In spite of the growing storm outside, the gloom within wasn't so bad, with gray light coming through the few small windows eating away at the shadows. Konstancji found himself growing more and more prepared, mentally, for the task at hand. Mingling with the shadows comforted him, bringing him to a state of melancholy reflection and intense brooding, which, in turn, fueled his desire to see his project to its completion.

The stairs curled in a long, ancient spiral, and the small, dark room he'd been using for his studio awaited him at the top. He entered and walked over to an unidentifiable lump standing in the middle of the room. It was covered with an old, discolored, and stained blanket, the heavy drapery hiding the more intricate shapes and silhouettes beneath. His tools lay on a nearby table along with a pile of rags. The rest of the room was bare, save for an antique chair that stood against the wall behind the cloth-covered object.

Sitters stayed there, patiently waiting while Konstancji labored on his artwork, ignorant of the masterpiece that was taking shape before them. No one had ever had seen what it was that had so consumed the young artist for so long now.

Konstancji worked on it even when they were gone, throwing himself at his masterpiece with every ounce of energy he had, chipping and shaving away excesses, polishing here and there, carving out details and subtleties, determined to capture in stone what he'd long considered to be perfection.

He worked at every waking hour with relentless focus, reluctantly breaking off for nourishment, hygiene, and occasional business dealings. He'd hired someone to oversee his finances, about which he didn't care a jot. He had more important things on his hands, after all.

His servant had been faithfully quiet about her young master's eccentric ways and had done a very effective job of deflecting curious inquiries about his activities. Even the sitters were thwarted with dismissive and vague replies, pushing them into a frustrated yet enthralled silence. Eventually they all understood well enough that their employer's drive was something sacred and, indeed, something that wouldn't stand to any inquiry, however innocent.

They never spoke of it after asking about it twice.

In fact, they never had the chance to go further.

Every single sitter hired for the job had died.

• • • •

AT NINETEEN YEARS OF age, Konstancji had about him an unusual mystique, an invisible cloak that shielded him from any deeper probing into his personal life. It was said that when a person happened to be in Konstancji's company, his mind would be lulled into a fogged, apathetic state, rendering his conversation superficial and limited to everyone else's lives or business—but never Konstancji's. At times, when the young man happened to be in a bigger group of people, that unusual protective haze would simply descend upon everyone, so that he'd be mingling and chatting, a faint, knowing smile on his face, while everyone else jabbered with hardly any understanding of what it was they were talking about. Once he left, the haze would fade slowly till it was gone, leaving people feeling a bit baffled and unable to remember much of what they'd talked about.

There were rumors about Konstancji's dead lover being a practitioner of the dark arts, that it was he who'd cast this strange shielding spell on Konstancji in order to keep the world away from their lives, but nothing had ever been proven.

Besides, there was also a practical side to all this.

Konstancji had inherited a good sum of money from his parents, though he never pursued the kind of lifestyle that one would have expected from one who'd been lavished with so much wealth. Money, it turned out, proved to be just as strong a shield against idle gossip as one cast by a warlock.

Whether by design or not, Konstancji was known to give generously to various orphanages, the first to open his purse strings whenever the need to arose, no matter how trivial. He'd never once offended anyone in either word or deed in spite of his characteristic distance and reserve—so much so that his odd habits involving his sculpting had been overlooked and regarded as the "workings of an artistic genius." The most amusing word that Konstancji had heard others use to describe him was "prodigy," given his talent in proportion to his age.

Besides, he paid his sitters well. It was generally thought that a man would be mad to pass up an opportunity to spend days locked away in the small room with him, watching him create something, watching his determination and passion for his work. Konstancji's obsession with his art meant working long hours, sometimes well into the night, as well as in terrible weather. Sitters who showed signs of doubt were paid more, and for their families' sakes, these young men braved dreadful conditions, even with their health deteriorating.

Grieving parents and siblings claimed to have begged their lost sons and brothers to stop before things went too far. But either those young men were determined to continue earning their generous compensation from Konstancji, or they were "bewitched" by their employer. The latter reason was always easier to dismiss, not so much for lack of evidence, but for the too-obvious fact that the village from where these youths came was miserably poor, and any acts of charity were greatly welcomed by the half-starved residents.

Old folks had their own ideas, of course, being of a more superstitious bent, but even they couldn't argue against their grandsons' generous pay and as such, thought to keep their dark mutterings to themselves. Younger members of their families amused themselves with their elders' grumblings, and before long, scandalous and shocking claims began to surface, with each gossiper embellishing his or her version till nothing but wild, outlandish—and, therefore, easy to dismiss—stories filled idle moments.

Every single one of the men, they said, had been "bewitched" by Konstancji to fall hopelessly in love with him, and when his employer repulsed him, he wasted away to his death, presumably from heartbreak. Outraged families of the deceased forced gossips into silence out of respect for the dead as well as for the young man who'd been so generous to them, even after their sons' deaths.

• • • •

KONSTANCJI TOOK HOLD of the blanket and gently pulled it off his work, resting his eyes on the figure that stood before him. He smiled softly.

"Hello, Ziven," he whispered, dropping the sheet to the floor and stepping forward to touch the cold cheek. "I missed you."

The statue never answered back and stared not so much at him but through him, lifeless eyes cast down and off to the side a bit, almost as though the figure were deep in thought, if not shyly receiving a well-deserved compliment.

Konstancji's hand trailed its way from the cheek to the carefully shaped and slightly parted lips, his fingers tracing the graceful contours and sending shivers through his frame.

"We don't have much time left," he added, now moving his hand from the statue's mouth to its neck to slide down its stone chest, abdomen, and side before moving to grasp a lifeless hand. "I'm sure you'll be thrilled to hear that. You must be very impatient by now."

Konstancji leaned his head against the statue's chest, pressing his ear against it in a vain attempt to catch a heartbeat as he continued to hold its hand.

"I've been patient enough," he continued, wrapping an arm around the statue's waist, fingers gently rubbing its lower back as though in comfort. "But even a saint has his limits."

The dull sound of approaching footsteps arrested his attention, and Konstancji hastily pulled away, grabbing the sheet from the floor and throwing it over the statue, tugging here and there to make sure that not an inch of it showed.

He stepped away and walked over to the solitary window behind him, taking in the dull light that filtered through the ancient glass. The sky was now a dark gray, the edges of the clouds fuzzy through the onslaught of rain that hammered against the roof, walls, and windows. Konstancji's ears perked up at the rhythmic, insistent sounds as he basked in the solace they afforded. He felt his agitation and excitement soothed until he was in control of himself once again.

The footsteps stopped right outside the door to the room, and a knock followed.

"Come in."

The door slowly opened, and the familiar figure of a young man emerged from the shadows beyond. Konstancji turned just in time and smiled at the newcomer as he took stock of the latter's weary and haggard form.

"How do you do, Borys?" he asked softly.

"I've been better."

"Come in, please. You're soaked."

Borys nodded and closed the door behind him before shuffling off toward the chair against the wall. There he doffed his ragged coat, which was drenched with rainwater. Konstancji watched him take his place in the chair, sitting himself down with a dejection that had grown more and more palpable every day that he'd spent time in the young heir's company. Exhaustion and crushed spirits racked his dwindling frame, reducing it to an abnormally delicate shape, thin and bony, and almost weightless.

There was intensity in Borys's eyes, however, one that was never snuffed out, and Konstancji coveted it, knowing that it was the final, elusive element he needed to bring his masterpiece to life.

He walked over to the shrunken figure.

"Borys," he said, his voice barely above a whisper. "I need you to sit up."

Borys sighed and shifted painfully around till his back was straight, but Konstancji could see the strain that position placed on his body. Borys' shoulders trembled from the pressure of being held up by weakened muscles, and his hands, grasping the armrests for support, were white-knuckled, the skin taut against the bones that pressed up on it.

Konstancji watched with a mixture of vague curiosity and pity, though he knew it couldn't be helped. He raised his eyes and met Borys's.

"Konstancji," came the thick whisper.

"No. Let's not start. It's pointless."

"You're killing me."

Konstancji suppressed a chuckle. "Killing you? How so?" He raised both arms up his sides, palms out. "What weapons am I using against you? Or do you mean poison? That's a serious accusation you're making, Borys."

"You know very well what I mean."

"You don't have to stay. I can get someone else."

"I can't leave," Borys stammered. "I can't. I have to see you—you know that. You won't let me be. You're making me return to this hellish place."

"Nonsense. I never keep you here against your will. I've always told you that you're free to leave if this becomes too much for you."

"You keep calling me back."

Konstancji offered a faint, expectant smile. "How so?"

"Here," Borys replied, pressing a bony hand against his chest. "I want to run, but I can't. You keep calling me back. I don't hear your voice, but I feel it here—and I'm lost."

"It's all in your mind, Borys. What you're talking about is no one else's influence but yours. You need to stop deluding yourself before it's too late."

"It isn't me," the ailing sitter replied a little sharply. "You *know* it isn't."

Konstancji's smile deepened, and he shook his head, raising a hand to run his fingers through wet, tangled hair. Borys offered him something, yes, but that wasn't enough. Nothing was ever enough when weighed against one who now lay under the blackened sky, his resting-place pummeled by its fury.

"I'm sorry," he replied at length. He trailed his hand down from Borys's hair to the damp skin of his cheek and felt the shiver elicited by his touch. He also caught the flash of deep revulsion and desperate need in Borys' eyes. "You know I can't."

"He's been dead for a year, Konstancji."

"Which makes things even more impossible between us."

Borys stared at him, puzzled and dazed, his breath coming and going in ragged gasps.

"He promised me," Konstancji said, his voice falling. "After a year, he said—on the anniversary of his death. He'll come back to me."

"That's impossible, and you know it."

"No. He lives, Borys. I can feel it. I can feel him everywhere in the house. And I don't mean traces of his past with me. I'm talking about *feeling* him—his presence. As if he's never really left. In the garden, I can feel him tending the roses. In the library, I can feel him sorting through books. In the parlor, I can feel him sitting beside me by the fire. In the bedroom, I can feel him lying beside me. His scent, his breath against my neck. Sometimes I hear his voice whispering to me." Konstancji's eyes sparkled with a wild urgency. "Sometimes," he continued, whispering fiercely, "I see him—I see his shadow everywhere—wandering around the house—the garden. Sometimes I feel it following me where I go. He's here. He never left me—in spirit at least. And he's waiting, biding his time."

His stricken companion stared at him incredulously.

"You don't have to believe me. I never expected you or anybody else to understand."

"He's dead, Konstancji. He's *dead*. Consumption took him from you. He wasn't ready, and you weren't ready, but it couldn't be helped. You can't fight Fate." Borys sighed, his breath hissing unevenly through cracked lips. "Let him go, for heaven's sake, and move on. There's so much more the world can offer you."

Konstancji laughed lightly and regarded his companion with a look of condescending pity. "Circumstances couldn't be helped, perhaps, but you underestimate the human will. Ziven promised that he'd return, he told me what

I needed to do and how it was all going to happen, and I promised to help him—welcome him back."

Borys shook his head, mouthing, "You're mad," and Konstancji leaned down to press his lips against his, a fleeting, idle kiss—gentle, amused...

...and deadly. He felt Borys open up and return his kiss, weak and desperate in his bid to savor the intimate connection, to savor a momentary victory in Konstancji's mouth, a hopeful lover watching all dreams and aspirations slip through his fingers and yet insisting on chasing after them despite the danger of yearning for Konstancji Michalovsky.

Konstancji allowed him to explore, surreptitiously sucking in some of Borys's breath as they kissed—just as he'd done with the others—before gently pulling away when he felt the other body drain itself of even more of its precious life force. He pushed Borys back, the scraping of the chair's legs sharp in his ears, until the chair stood pressed against the wall. It seemed appropriate, for Borys needed to be propped up even more by the ancient wallpaper and wood, his frail figure racked with soundless, desperate sobs. Konstancji offered another faint smile.

"Come now," he whispered. "You've got to stop. You know it's pointless going on about this. I don't love you. I can never love you—or anyone else, for that matter."

His companion remained silent, his gaze resting on him now, the sobs vanishing. Konstancji sighed and straightened up to walk back to the statue, taking his place before it and pulling up a part of the sheet to expose its front to him while keeping the back covered and so protected from Borys' fading gaze.

He stared up at Ziven's likeness and smiled. "Are you ready?" he murmured. "Borys is here to help."

He then picked up one of his tools and started to carve into the statue's eyes, gingerly chipping away, periodically stepping aside to refresh his memory of the intensity of Borys's gaze.

Minutes ticked by, and soon Konstancji had managed to sear the image of his sitter's eyes in his mind—so much so that he'd ceased to look at him, his attention now wholly on the statue as he sculpted. A flush crept up his cheeks as he worked, his eyes taking on a wild, crazed light as he struggled to capture that intensity, that passion, and trap it in stone.

It was a process he'd gone through countless times in the past with the other sitters. He'd had the blessed opportunity of capturing the air of wit and a zest for life from another young man, infusing that into his creation and watching the carved piece absorb it while the doomed sitter succumbed in much the same way that Borys was doing now. Another sitter offered him gentleness, while another gave him the gift of beauty. Each sitter provided him with varying essences that he devoured, absorbed, and nurtured with every scrap of his own native intensity, passion, and implacable willfulness, transferring them into the statue with every stroke of his tools.

They'd aid his lover's return. They'd mold the harsh, unyielding stone—render it more hospitable with essences that would enhance the dead youth's own once his soul laid claim to it. Every quality Konstancji had claimed and infused into the stone was one with which Ziven was blessed when he was alive. All Konstancji had been doing was ensuring that those magnificent qualities or essences wouldn't be lost in the process of helping Ziven come back to him. There was, after all, the risk of a soul being stripped of its original nature, in part or completely, as it journeyed back to the land of the living. It was better to overdo things—to take as much as Konstancji could from his foolish, obsessed admirers and guarantee that Ziven's nature would be intact.

As he worked, his fevered brain could barely make out the subtle yet unmistakable transformation that the statue was undergoing. Ignoring Borys, he threw himself into his work, half-aware of the slow changing of texture and color and warmth in the stone beneath his hands.

"Come back to me, Ziven," he whispered again and again as his hands worked more and more furiously. "I've been waiting a year. Come back to me."

He felt Borys's passion flow through his fingers—because his admirer, as he pined hopelessly for Konstancji's affection, had recklessly surrendered part of himself—part of his very soul—and had placed it in Konstancji's hands to be used at will. The sensation of warm electricity that defined that flow sent shivers of terror and excitement through the young artist, and he felt his spirits buoyed by the transference. He'd felt it several times in the past with the others, and he'd never grown tired of it, the thrill of both the sensation and the idea that his lover was benefiting from this transfer of life propelling him forward in a relentless push.

He savored his role as the conduit. It gave him an active enough part in bringing his beloved back to life, making Ziven's return to him all the sweeter.

An almost manic grin spread across his face as he finished the eyes, shifting his attention to minute details that needed to be finished and polished to further perfection.

"Yes," he hissed through clenched teeth. "This is beautiful. Just perfect."

He was now done except for one final thing to complete the picture: his beloved needed help in breathing. Konstancji leaned forward and craned his neck to press his lips against the statue's, flinching a little as he felt the chill and the stiffness of the stone against his mouth, his tongue gently molding itself within the small space he'd carved out between the statue's parted lips. He gently blew as he kissed, feeling the warmth of his breath envelop stone.

And as before, he felt Borys's essence flow from his mouth—the life-giving force he'd sucked out of his hopeful admirer—and mingle itself with his own breath to cocoon the lifeless lips.

He stopped and stepped back, eyes wide, face flushed, sweat dampening his brow. His gaze roamed desperately over the pale figure that stood before him, his breath caught in his throat, frozen by thoughts both terrible and wonderful.

The light dimmed further as the rain poured down in a heavier curtain, clawing at glass, wood, and brick and infusing Konstancji's spirits with an even more heightened sense of anticipation.

"Ziven," he said. "Come back. I'm here, waiting for you."

He made his desperate call again and again, his voice filling his ears with their hypnotic rhythm, severing all awareness of everything around him beyond the statue.

Then he saw it. Finally.

The movement was minute, but it was there. The white marble hand had moved, and he was certain that it wasn't a trick of the light. The fingers definitely twitched. Konstancji's heart raced, but he didn't move. At least not yet.

The chest heaved a little—a small intake of breath, clear and unmistakable. Those parted lips trembled, letting out a sudden gasp that could barely be heard. Then a faint rosy flush crept through the still figure, replacing white lifelessness with a soft flesh tone that spoke of warmth. Konstancji watched the transformation take place, doing his damnedest to squelch the maddening desire to run to the figure and hold it fast.

The figure's head moved, turning left and right slowly, the eyes blinking and taking on an odd, distant light—one often witnessed in those just waking up, confounded and lost, from a long, nightmarish sleep.

Its head raised itself up, the eyes—now taking on an odd shade of brown—gazing on the jubilant artist. A look of profound confusion first darkened that all-too-familiar countenance, but it was quickly replaced by one of recognition. What initial dullness there was softened to a tender light, and those eyes shifted to a more definite shade of rich earth. A light flush powdered the cheeks, and a deeper rosy hue tinted those lips.

Konstancji finally succumbed.

With a bright, irrepressible laugh of triumph, he rushed forward and threw his arms around the resurrected form of his lost beloved, feeling the transformation continue as his body pressed insistently against softening stone.

"I missed you," he cried, still laughing. He shut his eyes and allowed his hands to wander all over Ziven's back, desperate to feel familiar little details of his lover's person, taking in the unnerving coolness of the skin. It was much warmer than stone, yes, but still cooler than living flesh.

It mattered little to the triumphant lover.

A vague, guttural sound answered him at first as Ziven slowly found his voice. Konstancji knew well enough not to press for responses from his beloved, and he contented himself with clinging tightly and murmuring endearments over and over, while pressing as many kisses as he could against Ziven's neck or shoulders.

"A year's too long," he said breathlessly, his arms firmly wrapped around Ziven's shoulders, his face pressed against his neck. "It was miserable waiting, but I did everything for you—everything—as promised. I followed your instructions perfectly."

"Konstancji," Ziven finally whispered, his words halting and ragged as he held his lover. The sheet covering his nakedness slipped off his shoulders and collected at their feet in a crumpled pool of discolored fabric.

Konstancji smiled, tears gathering in his eyes. "I'm here. I've always been here like I said I would," he said. His senses, filled with nothing else but his lover, barely registered of the distant sound of quiet rustling and a dull thud. Outside the rain continued to hammer against the ancient, dreary house.

• • • •

THE SERVANT LEANED against the door, panting. She never liked walking up those infernal stairs, but her master spent much too much time in the little room at the end, and she was obliged to climb them in spite of her anxieties over their structural integrity.

She knocked once her breathing had steadied, and listened.

"Come in," a cheerful voice called out, and she turned the knob and pushed in, stopping dead in her tracks as her eyes scanned the room.

At one end of the room, in front of an old chair, Borys lay crumpled on the weathered floorboards. He was horribly pale and thin, his sunken flesh and near-emaciated countenance alerting her to the possibility of consumption, but she somehow couldn't dismiss the more fanciful probability that the unfortunate young man had fallen victim to his own passions for her master.

"They never learn, these young men," she sighed quietly.

In the center sat Konstancji, smiling brilliantly at her. Firmly cradled in his arms was her once-deceased master, who lay weak, trembling, pale and disoriented but certainly comfortable in Konstancji's hold. Ziven looked a touch bloodless, but she was sure that some nice, hot soup would bring the roses back to his cheeks.

She drew a sharp breath of relief as she curtsied to the lovers. It was good having the small household complete once more.

"Shall I prepare the table now, sir?" she asked Konstancji.

"Of course, thank you. Has a fire been started in the drawing room?"

"Yes, sir."

"Ziven needs his clothes laid out on our bed. I'll bring him there first before dinner."

"Will you need water and towels brought up?"

Konstancji nodded, warmth overcoming him. The old woman was always so sharp, was never a disappointment when it came to his and Ziven's needs. He felt remarkably fortunate. "That would be perfect, yes."

The housekeeper nodded in the direction of Borys's body. "What about him, sir?"

"We'll bring him downstairs once Ziven's washed and clothed. You'll have to call the doctor after we move him."

"Yes, sir."

She curtsied again before turning around to walk to the door. Then she paused, her hand resting on the doorknob, before glancing over her shoulder and fixing her gaze on Ziven. Had it already been a year? Time moved so fast, she thought.

"It's good to have you back, sir."

Ziven smiled wanly. "I never left."

She returned his smile and nodded. "Of course." Then she disappeared into the darkness of the stairway.

# The Dollhouse

At midnight the candles all burst into life, a thousand incandescent flames shredding the dead, icy darkness and blanketing the entire house with golden brilliance. Along with the twelfth doleful chime that rang from the antique clock, the candelabras came alive with a whispered puff, rousing the house's occupants in time for the Christmas festivities. It was a remarkable, magical tradition that happened every year.

With the candles' sudden vibrance, every inch of every room flared to life as well—walls covered with richly patterned paper, furniture of the best dark wood and the finest craftsmanship, some with the added elegance of brocade cushions, rugs of the most exquisite handcrafted detail, and all sorts of Christmas ornamentation that could possibly be imagined scattered throughout. Pine, holly, glass, velvet, silk—every wreath, swag, and fanciful shape filled the revelers' senses, offering them vivid reminders of the season regardless of where they turned.

From the great drawing room, the tiny four-man orchestra played lively country dances and stately minuets beside the tall and heavily-festooned Christmas tree. Good food from the formal dining room seemed endless, and wine flowed generously. It was, in almost every sense, the best, the most perfect Christmas celebration.

Life, however, does not subscribe to perfection, even in a grand house that seemed to embody it.

When midnight struck and the night was overcome by Christmas brilliance and cheer, the guests, having been roused from their sleep, welcomed the much-beloved holiday with voices raised in surprise, dismay, and outrage. And while it was tradition for the house itself to come alive on the twelfth stroke, it was also the revelers' tradition to spend the first half hour in utmost vexation and confusion, the next half hour in lingering resentment, and the rest of the celebration in a state of inebriated joy and contentment.

"What the devil?" a knighted old gentleman cried. He'd awoken to find himself in a very unhappy place—sitting on a stiffly cushioned loveseat beside a woman, who eyed him in equal dismay. That loveseat, moreover, was situated in the most private and intimate corner of one of the rooms downstairs, protected from everyone's view by a pair of strategically placed potted plants. For any couple who were fortunate enough to claim the spot, it was a most romantic place to be. Surely they deserved such an honor.

The knighted gentleman was very ungallant in the way he eyed his partner up and down with eyes flashing behind refined spectacles, the way his thick, white moustache bobbed up and down as he spoke, the way he unceremoniously tore his arm from the lady's grasp as though burnt. "Why does it have to be *you* every time? What the devil have I done to be punished like this?"

His partner was a short, plump, and haughty countess. Her hair was gathered in a painfully elaborate pile atop her head, held together by giant feathers and strands of pearls that festooned her crown like sparkling cobwebs. This remarkable mountain ensured an impressive vertical reach for her figure. She pulled her arm away as well.

"Heaven help me that I should be cursed to wake up with *you* in my arm, you ill-tempered old goat!" she retorted, snapping her fan open with an emphatic flourish. "I wouldn't stand within ten feet of you for any money!"

The ruddy-cheeked and blustery old knight spluttered. "I certainly would not give credence to the judgment of someone who looks like a disgraced actress!"

The countess gasped and let loose a torrent of furious insults as she stood up, punctuating that with a well-aimed smack of her fan against the old knight's head. Red-faced, the old knight leapt to his feet, stammering a string of incoherencies before turning around and storming away, but it did him little good. The countess, rage spiraling, followed her former partner through the bewildered crowd, gesticulating with her fan to emphasize her harsher points. The two chased each other from room to room. Their fellow revelers barely noticed the couple's shared insults though their voices were harsh and loud, at times sounding clearer than the orchestra's spirited strains.

Out into the hallway and then through the door of another grand room they went.

They marched past a young girl who was pushing her way through the throng. She was a delicate, pixie-like beauty in soft pink satin and with a head full of carefully shaped red curls. She glanced over her shoulder as she went, her eyes wide and searching and her mouth pressed into a thin, determined line. Whatever she was escaping from was nowhere within sight, for her look of expectation and mild dread relaxed, and she was negotiating her way toward the dining-room with a smile of relief that grew with every step taken.

Bursting into the dining room, she hurried over to one corner just behind the long banquet table. There two figures stood, lost in conversation. The girl grinned broadly at the sight.

"You made it here more quickly than I ever could," she laughed, and the two glanced up, returning her greeting with broad smiles of their own.

One of them was a Japanese youth of noble birth, resplendent in his robe of black and gold, his tall, sculptured headpiece further adding to his proud, royal bearing. With a careful yet graceful bow, he welcomed his young friend, who returned his greeting with a curtsy.

"It's far easier for me to have my way with my attendants than it is for you to escape yours," he replied in accented English that had always delighted his companions.

The young girl sniffed. "None of them wants me to set foot outside their little circle. They insist that I will be in grave physical danger once I venture out with an able chaperone, even more so if I wandered off on my own. Imagine that!"

"They're afraid that you'll break in two," the third person in their tiny group said cheerfully. She was a young girl who, unlike her companions, occupied a lower, humbler social rung. In truth, she was not much more than a servant, and her dull, patched-up rags and faded little bonnet said everything about her station. Her eyes were a brilliant blue, lit up with much wit, and if passersby were to take careful notice, they would catch sight of her hand which was, though lightly soiled from drudge work, firmly clasped between the Japanese prince's.

"Ridiculous," the little pixie retorted. "I'm not made of porcelain."

"Well, you *are* rather small," the servant girl said. "And very, very fragile-looking."

"Oh, lord, you sound like my insufferable chaperones."

And with that, she turned to the table, espied an open bottle of wine, and quickly claimed it for her own, taking a large, very unladylike gulp of its contents. Eyes dancing, she held the bottle up to her companions. "A drinking contest! I dare you both."

The lovers exchanged looks of amusement.

"Very well," the Japanese prince replied. "I've always been fond of European drink, and I know that my constitution and appetite are equal to westerners.'"

"A bottle for each," the servant girl added, breaking momentarily from her partner's grasp and claiming two more bottles from the table. "But perhaps we should go to the parlor or library for this."

The little pixie nodded enthusiastically. "And bring food with us, of course. We shall make a feast of it."

The Japanese prince took the proffered bottle and hastily gathered a wild mix of dishes from the table, using nothing more than his hands and arms, soiling his robes though he didn't seem to notice. The two girls did the same, chattering and giggling as they collected their treasure, with the servant girl using her apron as a makeshift basket and the little pixie her satin skirt.

"Hush, now, and run," the prince said, and the trio hurried off, a lively little group half-soiled by food and taking great pleasure in their freedom. Royal attendants and chaperones—it was all so silly and unnecessary.

"I wish I woke up with you two," the little pixie declared breathlessly as they vanished in the throng. "I hate having to fight my way out of my stuffy old corner just to be with my friends."

They left a scented trail of delicious food behind them, which a young student inhaled deeply as he passed their hurrying figures. He paused in his tracks and adjusted his cravat before scrutinizing himself in a nearby mirror. His features were refined—perhaps overly so, he always thought. He knew too well that he was expected to follow a completely different course upon his awakening, one that did not entail the special pleasure of an unusual romance. He'd always wake up in the company of a young lady who mirrored him in attractiveness and refinement, but Fate couldn't have made a graver error in judgment by throwing them together. Indeed, every time that odd, invisible force made itself known at midnight on Christmas Day, he found himself wandering away from the young lady.

"Please understand," she always begged with heartbreaking earnestness. "There's absolutely nothing wrong with you. I'm simply interested in someone else. I'm sorry, but I can't marry you. It isn't fair to either of us."

The student reassured her for several minutes that he wasn't hurt—could never be hurt—by her rejection before they parted ways. But he also realized that the next time midnight struck, he would still find himself at her side—or, rather, on his knees before her, a proposal of marriage poised on his lips, while she sat in languid splendor on a divan, ready to receive his offer with the gratitude and joy that was expected from a blushing bride-to-be. Unfortunately it couldn't be helped, and he knew it. At least—and here was some comfort—whenever he awoke, at least he was always given an opportunity to rectify the situation and find the person whom, he knew, was truly meant for him. It was an unusual attachment, but it was right. For a lovestruck boy such as him, it was quite *perfect*.

He walked briskly through the crowd, primping on occasion without even knowing it, the nervous anticipation growing with every step taken toward the conservatory. With the midnight hour came the reassurance that in the secluded room his beloved waited. It was a constant factor, in which he took great pleasure.

He didn't have to knock on the door. He simply turned the knob and slipped inside, his gaze falling on the lone figure sitting at the piano, idly tinkering with its aging keys. The piece sounded familiar, the student realized with a widening smile of relief as he closed the door gently behind him. He soon recognized an etude—of course, the one his beloved always played whenever the first hour of Christmas bloomed.

He didn't have to interrupt the music; he didn't even have to speak. All he needed to do was to take his place on the bench beside the solitary player and watch for several minutes in fond silence, his gaze fixed on the musician's long-fingered and skilled hands as they flew up and down the keyboard, coaxing some of the most intricately woven sounds he had ever heard from the antique instrument.

It was always the same, when midnight struck. When the music ended, he turned to his partner and smiled.

"You improve every time," he quipped, green eyes dancing as they took in the sight of a young man his age and his polar opposite in appearance.

"I practice before you come, of course." The dark youth shrugged wistfully. "I am always alone in this room when I wake up—I can't help but take to the thing that gives me the most relief."

The student grinned as he jokingly adjusted the dark youth's cravat. "Other than me, you mean."

"Other than you. And I assume that you—is she doing well?"

"My misplaced partner is now happily in the arms of our good host's footman, and she's exceedingly glad to be rid of me. They were always meant to be together. You know that, of course."

The dark musician—he was rumored to be of half-gypsy stock, but no one could really determine his birth—shook his head, laughing quietly. "She's not glad to be rid of you. The lady isn't as cruel as you make her out to be."

"No, she isn't," the student replied gaily, green eyes sparkling. "I was teasing you, as you know. You can be too serious at times."

"It's in my blood. You ought to know that by now." And with that, the dark youth turned to face the piano once again. "I also have a little divertimento that you might enjoy." He glanced briefly at his companion as the first few notes filled the room. "I'm certain you haven't heard this before."

"No, I can't say that I have," the student replied, and he fell silent as he listened. He remained still throughout the performance, even waiting till the final notes faded away. "It's a very pretty piece," he said at length, looking up and meeting the dark youth's anxious gaze. He smiled and shook his head. "I'm not teasing. You're remarkably talented, you know, and I wish you'd believe me when I say it."

The dark youth shrugged, looking sheepish. "I don't hear it enough."

"Well, you are. You're talented, you're talented, you're talented. There. Is that enough?"

The dark youth shook his head, bemused and relieved, and he smiled. It was always a bit of a challenge drawing that smile out of him, but then again, no one should be surprised. Waking up on Christmas and finding oneself alone and apparently ostracized from the rest of the company would dampen anyone's spirits. And if he happened to have the same shy, solemn nature as the dark youth, the effects would be worse.

The student decided to ensure that that rare smile would remain, and he leaned forward to press a kiss on the dark youth's mouth. When he pulled away, soaring with triumph at the look of amazement and delight on his beloved's face, he said, "Play that song you wrote for me."

The dark youth didn't need further encouragement. Elated and confident, he turned around and began playing.

The young student looked down on his beloved's hands and hummed along, perfectly in tune with a song he'd heard time and again. Every so often, the two would exchange playful grins, feeling more and more relaxed in the warmth and privacy of the conservatory. They couldn't be any luckier, considering where the other guests were forced to spend time with each other—crammed in the main rooms, barely able to move around without stepping on each other's feet. No one seemed to care much for the conservatory, but perhaps it would only be a matter of time before pairs of flustered lovers exiled themselves to the more remote sections of the house.

The student and the dark youth savored what private time they had together, grateful for every passing minute during which their sanctuary remained undiscovered. It was always so with them, when the clock struck.

As with other times, the two would spend most of the evening in the conservatory, content to converse and play music. Sometimes they moved away from the piano and onto the sofa nearby, and there they'd enjoy more physical pleasures in each other's arms.

This particular evening, the student felt more restless than he'd ever been. While he loved every moment they'd spent together in the conservatory, he thought that perhaps it was time for something different. The dark youth, despite the improvement in his mood, remained his tentative, pensive self, and something needed to be done.

"Wait," the student cut in, raising a hand. "Listen. A waltz."

He slid off the bench and offered a hand. The dark youth stared at it dubiously. "And? What of that? You know I can't dance."

"I always teach you, and you always enjoy yourself in spite of all your excuses." The student laughed again. "But let's try something different and join the others. Then after, we can eat ourselves to death. What do you think?"

The dark youth hesitated, looking momentarily panicked. "You're mad."

"I'm not! I won't abandon you—I swear."

The dark youth stiffened, looking doubtful and slightly hurt. "You always say that," he said, "and yet when I wake up, I'm always alone."

"You know I can't help that, and I always come to you. Please, can we at least try it just once? You don't have to like it, and if that's the case, we'll come back here and stay here for the rest of the night." The student gave his beloved's hand a gentle tug, hoping that it was also reassuring.

The dark youth pursed his lips as he mulled things over. His defenses were crumbling, and the student bent down and kissed him again, this time taking care to make it a touch more passionate and demanding. That seemed to work.

"Come along. The others are always pleased to see you, you know."

"Oh, very well. If I vomit all over you, you don't have anyone else to blame but yourself. Consider yourself warned."

The two emerged from their hideaway and moved through the crowds. Along the way, a lively conversation was drowned out—as usual—by the raucous sounds of holiday merrymaking. Protests from the dark youth, encouragement from the bright-haired student—everything melted in the cheerful cacophony of conversation, laughter, singing, and orchestral music. By the time they reached the drawing room, the lovers' heads would be swirling from all the talking. A good number of people addressed them as they went along, their attempts at conversation a jumbled mess.

"Hallo! Hallo! There you are!"

"What, more lessons, sir? Why insist on lessons? Look at me! I dance alone! Who says you need a partner every time?"

"Have a drink! Come, come, cheer up, young man! It's our time! This evening's ours alone!"

The young lovers were welcomed into the confused mix—a remarkable and altogether alien idea in an age where boundaries were usually severely defined.

The drawing room boasted an odd collection of dancers, certainly. It was, in fact, a bit haphazard. There were couples, looking mismatched in age or wealth, but who were immensely pleased with their situations. There were those of the same gender and those of the opposite. There were solitary dancers who simply twirled around the room, snaking their way through couples like colorful whirling dervishes. Some danced, holding aloft a bottle of wine, from which they'd take occasional gulps before bursting out in song or overly loud huzzahs. Sometimes the bottles would be passed around, with ladies and gentlemen alike helping themselves with no thought to decorum or even hygiene.

To any well-bred witnesses of the celebration, it would be a very scandalous sight. Perhaps the host or hostess's morals would be called into question. Perhaps judgment of the worst kind would be brought down on everyone's heads, given the inexcusable impropriety of their behavior. Perhaps the truly superstitious sorts thought a foul, wicked force was at work, possessing normal and decent creatures and turning them into a mockery of their true natures.

The young student and his beloved stumbled through the first two waltzes. "Stop being so nervous," he chided his partner.

"I'm not being nervous. I'm trying to remember what to do next," the dark youth grumbled as he frowned at his feet while noting the rhythm. For someone so talented in music, he was hopeless at dancing.

"Look at me. Up, up—yes, there you are. Just move with me, and everything will fall into place." The student held his partner's gaze as they danced in slightly clumsy circles around the room's perimeter. "And don't be so stiff."

"I'm trying, for heaven's sake."

Little by little, the dark youth's nervousness faded, and his hold on his partner relaxed. By the fourth waltz, they'd picked up a little speed and were cheerfully demanding another one whenever they whirled past the orchestra.

Beyond the drawing room, the rest of the revelers continued to untangle themselves from the confusion brought on by the midnight hour, and little by little, one by one, they found their rightful places—alone, in pairs, in groups. Once all was settled, a wave of relief rippled through the crowd, and the festivities truly began. Wine poured more profusely. Food was served in larger portions. Conversation and laughter grew till they rivaled the bright music coming from the little orchestra. Within two hours, more dancers would be assembled in the great drawing room, lost in quadrilles, minuets, and waltzes, while those who'd been dancing for some time would withdraw for some rest and conversation.

The student and the musician—like some of the other reunited lovers—crept out of the drawing room once exhaustion claimed them. From there they'd seek out a quiet little room on one of the upper floors and then spend most of the remaining hours in each other's arms before fixing themselves up again, going downstairs to enjoy what food was left, and then retiring back to the conservatory. Once there, they took off their shoes and sat on the rug before the hearth, enjoying the warmth and the food they brought with them. Their moods were much lighter than before, and lapses in conversation were spent in easy, companionable silence, with the young lovers gazing happily into the fire.

"Now this is definitely something different," the student said, grinning, as he faced the dark youth, the fire a protective—even possessive—barrier against the chill of the winter. "I think we just stumbled across a new tradition."

"Looking like an imbecile in front of the orchestra? It's a tradition I don't particularly care for," the dark youth replied, matching grin for grin, before biting into the piece of cake.

"With the right partner and enough practice, I'm sure you'll improve in no time." The young student chuckled as the dark youth rolled his eyes at him, his mouth too full for a proper retort.

Before long they were back on the piano, hammering out music and singing along, devouring every moment that was left to them. Miraculously, they remained alone in the conservatory, but they didn't care to wonder too much about that. Luck was on their side for one more night, and that was what mattered above all.

The candles continued to burn brilliantly till the dawn, when silence and sleep descended upon the festivities. The revelers, tired yet very content, took great care to be with their preferred company—or alone in some instances among those who were fiercely independent—when dawn broke, knowing too well what awaited them the next time the old clock mournfully heralded Christmas. There was always hope, of course, that when the candles once again burst into life, that they would find themselves where they *should be,* right where they stood before the charm was once again cast upon them—and not as they *tended to be,* which was separated and miserable.

· · · ·

IT WAS A HOPE THAT was not shared in the Trowbridge household. In truth, it was a constant source of vexation for the youngest daughter, for she knew that her parents would never approve of it. The poor child was sometimes scolded for her apparent caprice despite all her tearful denials.

"Where on earth do you get these ideas from? This is outrageous!" Mrs. Trowbridge demanded more than once as she loomed above the cowering child, eyes flashing, hands on her hips. "Are you testing us?"

"No, I'm not," the little girl insisted. "They were all like this when I woke up."

"Ah, now it's lies, isn't it? I'll have to talk to your father about this. Now put your dolls back in their proper places."

Once or twice, the little girl had been sent to bed without supper, and she cried herself to sleep.

On Christmas morning, therefore, she learned to rise very early—well before her family—and hurry to the corner of her room, where her beloved doll-house stood. She shivered in the cold, but she ignored it, the fear of her parents' anger proving to be a much stronger force than the sting of winter. Her dollhouse was a large, gorgeous thing, boasting the most intricate details from roof to wall to window to floor. Furniture, candelabras, wallpaper, and even food and drink were all crafted by the best artisans around, and no expense was spared by Mr. and Mrs. Trowbridge. Why should they skimp, after all? They were wealthy, and they doted on their children, demanding nothing but the best for them.

It was an heirloom piece, handed down from generation to generation, but the interior details and the furniture and extra pieces were current. The dolls came with the dollhouse, and for them, a lot of trouble went into their clothes and appearance, for each generation of little girls wished their dolls to reflect their time. What might have been fashionable a generation ago was now inappropriate. No one in the household remembered where the dolls and the dollhouse came from originally.

The dollhouse's history, however, hardly mattered to Mrs. Trowbridge's youngest daughter, who met each Christmas morning with so much dread and not the natural delight that all children felt on such a special day. Peering inside, the little girl saw her fears confirmed and burst into tears, and she sank to her knees.

"Why can you not behave?" she sobbed. "Mama will be so cross with me when she sees all of you like this, acting like barbarians. You know how you should act! Why do you keep doing this?"

Knuckling away her tears, she rearranged the pretty little porcelain dolls, placing them in their proper places as directed by her parents. The distinguished older couple—the knighted gentleman and the extravagantly dressed countess—belonged together because they looked the part of a happily married pair. They also had about them an air of dignity and wisdom, which made them quite perfect together, and setting them down on the loveseat, protected by the potted plants, was ideal.

The delicate-looking girl in the soft pink dress was placed back in her assigned corner, where she could be protected by a group of older people—a protection she certainly needed, being such a pale, fragile creature. It was a strange thing that her chaperones couldn't seem to keep her within their sight, and that darling little pixie-like girl always found herself in very questionable—not to mention coarse and inappropriate—company.

The Japanese prince ought to have stayed with his entourage—aloof, untouchable, and proud, for that was how royalty acted. Who'd ever heard of a prince dismissing his attendants and wandering off to mingle with those who were clearly beneath him? The servant girl—shame on her. She belonged in the kitchen, scrubbing pots, and nowhere else, for she didn't dress the part of a bright, sophisticated lady. That she would consider herself good enough to converse with a prince as well as a refined young woman—what presumption!

The handsome young man with the golden hair should never wander far from his beloved, for they looked quite lovely together, and he ought to be proposing marriage to her like the great romantic that he was. It was rude and ungentlemanly of him to abandon the young lady the way he did, and worse, he'd abandon her to the attentions of a wretched footman. The little Trowbridge girl wasn't sure if the man in the company of that elegant lady was, indeed, a footman, but it hardly mattered. He wore a servant's livery, and like that presumptuous maid, he should be dispensing his duties as a servant, not chasing after young ladies who were his superiors.

And as for the strange, dark-featured youth—seeing as how he was a mystery—very likely a mongrel in terms of birth—he really ought not to be with the others. Mrs. Trowbridge had long determined that the dark youth was a nameless guest of no worth who should be isolated in the conservatory, for that room was well out of everyone else's way. He could make use of the piano, to be sure, to keep himself occupied during his solitary confinement. It didn't feel right for him to mingle in lovelier, more superior, company. Besides, who would want *him?* He was dark, he had about him a melancholy air that didn't fit the glittering brilliance of the dollhouse and its occupants, and he didn't seem to have a pedigree of any kind.

So why would that handsome young man with the golden hair end up in the same room as that dark youth every single time? He had the clear advantage of a pretty bride-to-be, and yet, there he was, befriending another boy who didn't belong anywhere. It made no sense whatsoever, the same way that the shocking pairing up of the other dolls made no sense.

The little girl repeated all these points to herself as she placed her dolls in their rightful positions. "Mama tells me that this is how you ought to be," she added once she had done, shaking a scolding finger at her collection. "And Mama is always right."

Once satisfied with the way the dollhouse's world looked, she tiptoed back into her bed, teeth chattering, skin prickling, and crawled under the thick bedclothes. Though there was still plenty of time before the rest of the household would begin to stir, sleep remained elusive, and it was all she could do to burrow under the covers and wait, her earlier distress slowly giving way to the brighter promise of gifts and good food later.

Christmas and the porcelain dolls, however, refused to listen to anyone's pleas—year after year—even when another little girl took possession of the dollhouse from her mother.

# The Winter Garden

I held Adrian the first time we met. We were on the ground, grappling, bruises on our faces, dirt and debris on our hair and clothes. I'd never been one for confrontations, let alone physical fights. Were I to be pitted against the weakest schoolboy, I'd be the one to fall first. I might even provide a source of entertainment with a show of the most ridiculous efforts at fisticuffs. I never learned how to fight, given the fact that I spent more time lying on my back, leveled by a recurring illness, than playing with friends and enjoying activities that healthy, robust boys could do with ease. But he provoked me, and I was forced to defend my honor—all fifteen years of it.

Adrian, exhausted by my pitiful efforts, held me tightly against himself to avoid being struck further. I was left to flail about, my fists meeting with nothing but coldness and stray leaves that drifted with the currents. I don't know how long it until exhaustion claimed me, but it must have been a while, for Adrian chided me over it more than once afterwards.

"One would have thought that you were possessed by the devil, the way you were carrying on," he snorted, dragging a hand through unruly gold hair, blue eyes darkening with impish pleasure as he looked me over in the way only he could. The child of decadence, I'd always thought, regarding the son of privation.

"It wasn't my fault."

"Well, I suppose you do what you can to protect your territory."

. . . .

MY ENTIRE EXISTENCE was held firmly within the circle of weathered stone that walled my parents' extensive garden. My earliest memory of life was watching birds sail from the uppermost branches of an oak tree toward the ivy-choked wall, vanishing past it, never to be seen again. I was never allowed to venture beyond the garden walls without being hemmed in on each side by my parents. All activity was restricted by their indulgent anxiety over my health, and when moving about in the city, they took care to lead me by my arms here and there.

The garden became my world, and there I spent most of what time I had free from my tutor's company. All interaction with the world happened between the rusted bars of the small garden gate at the north wall. I'd press my face between the bars to watch time and the world take another step closer to infinity while the garden was left static, and before long I'd earned the reputation of the Garden Ghost among the neighboring boys and girls. Those who thought it worth their time to converse with me claimed that I looked too pale and melancholy—like an abandoned specter—whenever I took my place behind the weathered iron. But for all their sympathies, none was inclined to do something about it, opting to leave me at the gate while they carried on with their business and their play, vanishing behind passing carriages and carts.

Adrian appeared one day, no different from those birds that strayed inside the garden from unknown distances. While I stared through the bars, a pale figure sauntered toward the gate and startled me out of my self-pitying stupor.

"Good day," he said, bending closer and narrowing his eyes for a better look. "Are you a prisoner?"

"Well, no. I live here."

"What's the difference?"

"I haven't done anything wrong."

He took a step closer till our faces were nearly touching between the bars, and I could feel his breath fanning me. He smelled of fruit and wine, and I was repulsed; debauchery and all sorts of drink-associated sins crossed my mind. He was one of those unprincipled, dissipated wretches my parents had warned me against, I thought. And yet I held on to the gate and stared back, amazed.

"Do you know how sad and puny you look?"

"Is that an improvement from looking like a ghost?"

Adrian chuckled then winked. "Well, well—it's a pretty prospect that you have," he said as he straightened up, fixing his gaze behind me. He even craned his neck and stood on tiptoes in order to enjoy a more sweeping view of the garden. "I believe that I'll take advantage of your good humor and admire your little garden more closely."

I blinked as he moved off to the side. "I beg your pardon?"

Adrian ignored me and scaled the northern wall, undaunted by the height, not at all cowed by the danger posed by my parents' vigilance. Somehow his hands and feet found sufficient purchase in the mossy, ivy-choked, and weathered rock, and he climbed with hardly any effort, it seemed. Like the birds that flew out, he sailed over the half-crumbling barrier though, unlike them, he traveled the other way, entering a scene of waning warmth and the initial days of cold and desolation, not flying away from it.

This violation sparked our fight. I knew my limits all too well, however, and concession was my only way out, for Adrian didn't show signs of leaving.

. . . .

AFTER THE FRUITLESS fight, he explored the garden with my help, the ease with which he plunged into unknown territory—almost claiming it for his own—indicated a boy who'd never been denied anything, and I was suddenly demoted to nothing more than a confused guide.

"By God, you're a lucky fellow!" he declared at the end of our exploration.

"I don't feel like one."

"Why not? This is a damned sight better than what I have!"

I stared at him. "What do you have?"

"Everything," he laughed, his voice edged with bitterness. When he paused, he rested his hands on his hips and took a more lingering and wistful inventory of the garden. Then he added in a tone that was edged with a great deal of regret, "Everything."

"I'd love to have everything. Well—anything other than what I have now, at least."

He merely rolled his eyes at me. "You must be one of the most ridiculous people I know," he said, reaching out to pull some dead leaves from my hair. Bruised and bewildered, I took that as a compliment—and then told my parents that I'd fallen off a tree later that evening. No one suspected a thing, and my mother fussed as expected. I fretted, though, over the deceit, wondering if lying to my parents would turn into a habit.

Adrian scaled the garden wall several more times afterwards in spite of my warnings of parental wrath, and he once retorted, "I don't care to hold conversations through iron bars, you thick-headed baby."

Our friendship developed from that point, an odd, symbiotic bond in which desire for an outside connection melded with a craving for an escape. We also managed to keep a respectful distance from each other's private lives, our conversations skirting the edges of outlawed subjects and following superficial lines that revealed nothing—and yet everything—about ourselves. More often than not, he'd appear smelling of drink, his arrogant charm dependent on the strength of his scent, and fear of offending him kept me silent on the matter.

When he spoke of his friends, I wouldn't hear it and sulked. "Are they all you can talk about?" I asked, watching him climb a tree with little trouble. I could never follow him because my strength tended to flag rapidly despite my efforts at taking care of myself and getting plenty of rest. "What's so special about them, anyway?" I glared at the tree's roots before me, not at all caring whether or not he heard.

When he sang the praises of girls, I felt my stomach tighten and quickly shifted the subject. When he joked about boys with whom he'd enjoyed an afternoon of riding in spite of the weather, I distracted him with odd bits about the garden. He found my jealous displays amusing but eventually lessened such talk.

Adrian moved the way he spoke—flitting lightly and easily from one point to another, leaving me rooted in the middle of a path, blasted on all sides by the chill winds and unsure of how to follow.

I couldn't touch him—hold him down—if I tried. He always grazed past me, barely disturbing the grass and low branches, and before I knew it, he'd be gone, exploring the higher branches of a tree or lost in the taller shrubbery. And all I had would be a faint whiff of boy and sweat (sometimes of wine), which kept a firm hold on my mind, and the sound of his voice coming from somewhere, mocking in its indeterminable direction.

"Why can't you stay still for two seconds together?"

"Why should I?"

I scowled at a pair of well-shod feet hanging down and swinging lazily amid the shadows of a nearby tree. I wished that I could leap up and take hold of them, pulling their insufferable owner back down to earth with me. "Because it's rude to push your way into my garden..."

"Your parents' garden, you mean."

"...and then refuse to hold a proper conversation with me."

He laughed, those well-shod feet convulsing slightly. "I just caught you in a lie," he cried. "I've had several conversations with you face-to-face, and don't deny it."

I toed the ground, sighing. "That's no excuse. If you refuse to speak with me through the gate's bars, I refuse to speak with you, hiding up a tree like this."

"I never told you not to follow me."

"You know very well that I can't."

There was a brief pause. "Oh? Why? Because you're too cowardly to climb?"

"I'm not a very good climber, is all," I replied, still toeing the ground. "Go ahead and ask my mother how many times I've hurt myself trying. I don't have the strength. I never had and never will."

There was another pause, one slightly longer. "It's good that you stopped trying, then. Swear to me that you won't try anymore."

He sounded so solemn and so sincere that I looked up at the tree, searching for his face, surprised and a little confused. "If it pleases you, I swear it."

I didn't feel any guilt that my mother had asked me the same thing in the past, but I brushed her off with a complaint of being suffocated. "Please stop treating me like a baby, Mama!" was my usual retort, which usually led to emotional words exchanged between us. Those quarrels always ended with me storming to my room and then slipping out of the house when I felt it was safe. With Adrian, I never thought twice about promising him anything.

We spent the rest of his visit in companionable silence; I braved the cold like I always did, huddled against the base of Adrian's tree while he sat above. When I appeared at the dinner table, I declared that I spent my afternoon walking around the garden, hence my flushed complexion.

"My dear Nicholas, you shouldn't spend so much time outdoors, seeing how badly the weather's turning," my mother said.

"Exercise is good for me."

"During warmer months, yes, but not now. My goodness, I thought you'd be spending more time in your room, reading."

I shrugged impatiently. "I'll wear my thicker coat next time."

My parents weren't convinced. I was to limit my wanderings outdoors for the rest of the season, withdrawing into the shelter of the house on my parents' orders once they'd judged the weather too harsh for my weakened constitution to withstand. I took umbrage at that, claiming that they knew nothing of what I could and couldn't endure. But as it stood, I was the child, and they were the authority. I took my complaints to Adrian, whose visits I'd learned to expect—no, look forward to—with growing impatience.

He didn't take to my grievances very well. "For God's sake, count yourself lucky for having parents who care," he retorted, grimacing at me before stalking off through the tall shrubs as though he were intent on disappearing in their midst. If he wished to leave me behind by doing so, he was greatly mistaken. I followed him like an affection-starved puppy.

"What, and you haven't?"

"I have parents who live and breathe, yes, but even if I didn't, I wouldn't see much difference in my life."

I was incredulous. "You're given everything—much more than I can ever hope to have. Why are you carrying on like this?"

"Don't presume you know all there is to know about everything outside your little cloistered world," he replied frostily.

"I don't understand you," I said, panting, and he finally stopped when we reached the opposite corner of the garden.

"I never asked you to." Then he softened, looking exhausted and older when he turned to face me. "I came here for a reason, you blockhead. Be kind to us both and preserve yourself the way your parents are trying to preserve you."

"And remain stunted and ignorant for the rest of my life, you mean?"

"I'd give anything to be as ignorant as you. Since it's far too late for that, I suppose I'll do anything to keep you as you are instead." He gazed at me for a moment, the silence weighing heavily, a strange light in his eyes. I thought that he wanted to tell me something more, but if he did, something kept him from saying those words, and he satisfied himself instead with a light touch of his fingers against my cheek. The scent of wine was particularly strong on him that day.

"If it's any comfort, I get sick too often to stay in school, and Mama wants to hire a tutor instead," I said. "I mean, I've had someone teach me before, but Mr. Thompson had to sail to America last month, and we've yet to hear from someone new."

Adrian listened, a wistful smile forming. "A selfish part of me hopes that you hire no one else, but I know it isn't fair."

I confess to feeling half-resentful, half-flattered, by his mania at seeing me as untouched by the outside world as the garden, my vanity stoked by the thought of my serving an invaluable purpose to him.

Adrian told me once that I reminded him of a tree. Perched comfortably on a low branch, he endeared himself further by feeding my mind with all sorts of fantastic images I'd never before associated with myself. Sometimes, he said, I seemed to become the trees. He could see the roots sprouting from my shoes, digging deeply into the grass—my skin turning brown and cracked and moss-eaten—my hair bursting into a thick cluster of leaves that broke off, one after another, and were driven before the winds to parts unknown. Eventually they gathered somewhere, falling victim to time till they disintegrated, and part of me was gone forever.

The elegiac nature of his analogy escaped me then. My naïveté had fixed me on only one line of understanding, my infatuation refusing me a wider scope. I'd fallen in love with the pretty images with which he compared me, and I kept my mind on the romantic meaning of his descriptions.

"So I'm constant like the trees," I said, grinning and blushing, "which makes a great deal of sense, really, seeing as how I'm quite stuck in this garden."

"Yes, you're constant."

I decided to try my hand at pretty imagery as well. I leaned against the tree, gazing up at him and sensing his restless energy radiating outward. I couldn't help but smile. "You're the wind, then," I said. "You're restless, you're always moving about, talking and talking, and you know so many things. It's like you've picked up all these stories from your travels all over the world."

"That's rather poetic of you. What a pair we make, and what sentimental inspiration we serve," he replied, chuckling. "Here—an ode of the wind and tree."

I encouraged his visits (not that he needed it) and continued to brave the worsening temperatures till snow began to dust the garden.

My parents had long curtailed my activities, but I'd also learned to find ways of escaping their vigilance, my confidence bolstered further by my growing comfort in deceit. Our house was large, our family tiny, and we only had two servants working for us. Mama and Papa were almost always away, visiting friends or having lunch or tea elsewhere, and with the servants busy with house-work, slipping out and returning before my parents came back proved to be a great deal easier than I'd first expected. As long as I was back in my room, bundled against the chill and enjoying a book by the time they returned, everything was fine.

That Adrian sought me out in spite of the coming winter and in spite of the risks taken on his health was incentive enough for me to make my own sacrifices. He was rich and spoiled, the smell of wine intensifying almost every time he appeared, often rendering conversation almost impossible. I was amazed that he'd managed to scale the walls without a single fall. Determination or desperation, perhaps, forcing his mind to clear itself till he reached the garden and was once again at my side.

I saw myself as his savior and refused to deviate from my own task of offering him comfort. There was a vindicating, euphoric thrill in being chosen to rescue another, to render his existence more palatable and more hopeful if only for an hour. I was pleased—honored. Adrian had turned the garden, the lifelong symbol of my deficiencies, into a haven I willingly embraced. There was conversation; there was life regardless of its shadows; there was a link to the outside world that neither my parents nor my former (or even future) tutor could ever give me. I was correct in my assessment of his character; Adrian was the wind.

I ignored the fever when it bore down on me and for a few days put up a cheerful, lively front before my parents and the servants. The thought of knowing something they didn't lent me a sense of power, and I clung to it—found strength in the thrill of subversion and secrecy.

"See, darling? Now you know things would have been much, much worse if you subjected yourself to the cold air," Mama often said, tempering her victory with a sweet smile and a kiss on my head. If only she knew.

By the time Adrian and I found each other again in the garden, I'd already grown far too tired from my masquerade within doors as well as my recent illness, and I was forced to shorten our time together. But we continued to walk the same frozen paths, pick our way past the same snow-covered shrubs, take our place on the same ice-powdered trees, with Adrian sitting on a branch and I huddled on the ground below him.

I forced him to wait much longer than he'd been used to one afternoon because a wave of dizziness overpowered me, and I needed to wait out its effects. He looked dreadful when I finally reached his side.

"I'm only a bit late," I panted, shamefaced and shivering. "I'll never leave you, you know. I swear I never will."

Adrian had to let a minute run its course while staring at me in a mixture of resentment, fear, and gratitude before he said anything in return. "I know you won't. I'm glad." He rested a hand against my cheek and smiled but said nothing more.

He looked and behaved more calmly as the days passed, the stench of wine fading at last. He seemed even pleased—assured. He continued to call me names, claiming superiority in age since he was two years older than I was, though they remained playful marks of affection. I didn't care either way so long as he was there, and I took them for compliments. His conversation, his mere presence—held me together through those hours spent wracked with a mild fever.

The last time we parted ways, he smiled and said, "I won't be seeing you again—at least for a while. I'm off to Canterbury with Papa. Stupid, trifling business, really." Then he embraced me the way he did when we fought: a tight circling of arms around my shrinking chest till I could barely breathe.

He was larger than I, and I couldn't see much over his shoulders save for snow and calm everywhere—a silence in the midst of the Christmas frenzy outside the walls. I held him as tightly as I could, pressing my nose against his shoulder and breathing in his scent, my heart dying. I pressed a kiss against his shoulder just as he pulled away, and I followed him back to the gate, watched him climb up the wall, and then take one of his hands in mine between the gate's bars.

"I'll be here when you come back," I said, braving a smile. "You know I never leave this garden."

"I know—like a tree."

• • • •

MY GRIEF CRIPPLED ME though I managed to contain it, at least in company. That evening I collapsed at the dinner table. My charade crumbled though no one knew how long I'd been ill, and I refused to admit anything even then, when circumstances had grown dire.

The progress of my illness had always been difficult to track, let alone put into words. I drifted in and out of sleep and found that being awake was far worse than the isolating oblivion of rest. I heard nothing but a fading montage of voices around me, and I kept my conscious thoughts on the garden, its winter cloak, and Adrian. In time I was roused, if only briefly, by a sharp pain on my arm, the warm trickling of corrupted blood, and the familiar voices of the surgeon, who spoke in grim murmurs, and my parents, who pressed him with questions that barely broke through the thick fog in my mind. Another tiresome process of being bled, I thought, and I slipped back into the night.

I don't know how long it took me to wake up again; I can't even recall when it happened. All I know now is my standing at the window of my room all of a sudden, gazing at the winter garden below and marveling at its serene beauty. I felt quite good and not at all chilled and weakened, and I stared out the window filled with melancholy thoughts of Adrian. I don't even remember how I left the house, but I did by blinking once, twice, and I was wandering through the snow with the bright sky above, feeling marvelously relaxed and calm. The garden itself was heavenly, a peaceful landscape of snow hiding the coming Spring, trees and plants biding their time in winter sleep.

My time since then had been difficult to track, no less difficult than the progression of my last illness, but I didn't mind and had long since resigned myself to retiring to my dark and empty house after my walk in a garden that never seemed to pull itself out of winter. As I stood before the back door, sweeping my gaze across familiar windows and the gabled roof, I realized that I was alone. I knew it, understood it, accepted it with the passivity and indifference that only fate could instill in a person whose will had been subverted.

My family was gone. The servants as well. Simply looking at the windows from the outside told me that much. The curtains were all taken down, and when I entered the house, I gave the interior a good deal more attention that I did when I first awoke, and I saw that the house—my house—had been emptied of furniture, knickknacks, and pictures hanging on the walls. Only shadows filled every corner now, and I knew what had happened since I last closed my eyes against the world, desperately ill and being bled by the surgeon. As it stood, though, a certain apathetic calm had taken over, for what else was there for me to do? I closed my eyes as I stood in the empty drawing room and sighed.

Time moved forward for everyone else, but in my new existence, I never felt it, though I could see its progression.

I noticed the trees and the shrubbery change though the garden remained snow-kissed, which I thought rather quaint. A couple of trees vanished, and new potted plants replaced them. New pathways appeared here and there, and on occasion, I heard the murmur of unfamiliar voices. I caught sight of a person or two sometimes, but I kept myself in the shadows or, if caught in the middle of a path, stepped aside as these strangers walked past, ignoring me. Once in a while, though, I'd be noticed without being seen. The person would realize that he wasn't alone, and he'd stop in the middle of his tracks, glancing around and looking bewildered—even unnerved—before moving on. Sometimes at a faster and slightly agitated pace.

One time I stood before my bedroom window and locked gazes with a woman who stood outside and right below me, bundled against the chill, a look of stricken horror on her face. But all I did was blink, and I was once again in the garden, and I could hear her panicked voice calling out to someone in some part of the house about seeing "the poor dead boy haunting the back room" again. Sometimes I took my place at the iron gate, which was now so weathered that I refused to touch its bars. Passersby slowed down, looked at me—looked *through* me—the familiar expression of disquiet and uncertainty shadowing their features before walking on. I even recognized some of them from my childhood, looking older every time.

Adrian returned to me as he'd promised, but it had been too late.

I saw him creep into the garden every so often, looking at least a year older and more worn down every time. It didn't matter to me then, and it doesn't matter now, for I can still see him whenever he chooses to come and remember the past. At times he'd carve the year on his favorite tree. We were at 1822, it seems—seven years since he last embraced me. I expected him to carve a few more.

He'd stopped scaling the garden wall and has long taken to using the iron gate, whose lock he disabled. He'd stopped climbing trees and simply sat on their twisted roots as I used to do, and I took my place beside him or before him—wherever I pleased. I'd watch the muted light in his eyes as he spoke aimlessly, his words clearly meant for no one but me, and I'd feel—as I always did in his company—unequivocally loved.

"Someday perhaps you'll forgive me for doing this to you," he'd always say. "It's my fault you got sick. I shouldn't have kept you outside for so long, even when I knew that you weren't well." Sometimes I'd laugh, and I think he heard me. He'd hold his breath and listen before carrying on, a smile—vacant and distracted—broadening. It became a familiar pattern for us, this one-sided conversation. "But I realized that someday this garden wouldn't be enough to contain you, and you'd be off. Gone. You'll move away, be sent elsewhere, wherever it is your family decides to take you. I couldn't bear the thought, and—how long can one cling to what he wants?"

Too long, it seemed, and I speak for both of us. The light in his eyes would intensify, grow wilder. One might say that he'd gone quite mad. "Do you know what's worse? That I was too much of a coward to follow you when I found out. I'm so sorry. I just wanted to spend as much time as I possibly could with you."

And where's logic in all this? I'm forever frozen at fifteen years of age though I feel much older every time I awaken; my sentiments remain impervious to reason though it might flicker to life during moments such as this, when I look back with regret. But the fiery, irrational brilliance of a boy's first love remains unquenched, and I forgive him every time I set eyes on him. If allowed another chance, I know I'd be resorting to all sorts of childish trickery to find my way back to his side, blindly sacrificing everything for him. Then I'll still awaken someday to discover myself bound to the garden, waiting and searching.

"But you always get what you want," I'd reply in hopes of comforting him, and sometimes I'd brave a kiss on a cold, sunken cheek. I think he felt me since he'd cry when I touched him.

With age comes infirmity, and I'm blessed to see time creep into my little patch of static existence with every visit he makes. All the same, I also bear witness to the ravages of a burdened conscience, and I know that it won't be long before I'll have my way as well. On his final visit to the garden, which I expect to be soon, he'll keep his place at my side, and the perpetual winter won't feel so desolate.

No, I'm mistaken. It's now. He's here. See, he's just scaled the wall, and he's leaped down. My breath catches in my throat as we look at each other, my heart soaring at the sight of Adrian in the bloom of youth—handsome and healthy and moving like the wind, looking exactly the way he did when we first met. He laughs when he sees me, of course, and after a long embrace, we hurry through our garden hand in hand, bursting with questions and stories for each other, for we've entire lifetimes' worth of talking to do and an eternity to do so at our leisure.

# The Knight

The worst thing would have to be the people's faces—the mingled looks of terror and despair on those whose child had been chosen and relief, joy, and pity on those who'd been spared. I'd seen them all—twelve times a year for four years—I'd seen them all.

They were my subjects, people who depended on my family's benevolence and my father's wisdom and sense of justice. In us they'd placed their trust and loyalty, unwavering and blind to the very end. They were unschooled, ignorant, their dependence on us child-like to the point of absurdity at times. But they didn't know any better. Their innocence had spared them the bitterness of the truth, and the burden fell on us—those of us close enough to my father to know his deeper desires and intentions—to bear the weight of the complete incongruence of his words, his actions, and his heart.

I'd long wondered why I was always spared the misfortune of being chosen. Twelve times in a year, I was placed on equal footing with my peers—standing on the platform with the rest of my family while one of my father's ministers would pull out a black wooden chip from the chest, watching and waiting with bated breath for the next victim's death warrant to be proclaimed before the entire kingdom.

For four years—since I was thirteen—my name had never been called. Month after month, year after year, I had to stand by in nervous anticipation before falling into a state of shocked relief and overwhelming sadness and pity for the poor family whose child had been chosen for the sacrifice.

"Bronwyn, daughter of Cuthbert," the minister would say, the sound of his voice heavy on the terrified crowd.

A gasp would ripple through the huddled mass as parents, brothers, and sisters turned to each other and held each other tightly, prayers of thanks on their lips for being granted mercy this time around. In the meantime, Bronwyn and her family erupted in desperate tears, holding each other close as well but for different reasons.

The drawing of Bronwyn's lot would signal her final day spent in her family's company. From this point, she was escorted to one of the castle towers, where she was cleaned and dressed in white as though a young bride, a garland of wildflowers perched almost mockingly on her head. She was then carried off by horse with an impressive escort to the cliffs just beyond our kingdom's borders. There, on a gigantic boulder that had been split in two by lightning, she was shackled and then abandoned—to wait for her "groom," who was expected to make his appearance at the expected hour.

The groom was a dragon, her wedding-bed a pyre.

Early the following morning, my father's soldiers would return to the cliffs to confirm the sacrifice and come back to us with tokens of Bronwyn's demise—a tattered piece of fabric, a stray flower, a ring—anything that used to belong to her was produced, partly burned and, in some cases, smeared with blood.

The kingdom then mourned, the dragon left us in peace for another month, and all went back to its regular rhythm. Men and sons labored, wives gave birth, daughters cooked and cleaned.

I, on the other hand, could never find any vestige of normalcy in my existence. For four years, I walked my father's hallways, weighed down by memories of the sight of my subjects' helpless terror and their children's stoic resignation to their fate. They never had much, my people. They were miserably poor, barely managing to survive on whatever meager income they'd managed to earn from their labors.

And for them to be subjected to this grisly lottery in order to pacify a monster that had haunted our lands for as long as anyone could remember—that was, in my eyes, one step gone too far. Misery piled atop misery—no one deserved it, especially these poor wretches, who had done nothing wrong to warrant this punishment.

I waited for my turn. Fool that I was, I believed in my father just as my people believed in him. Time and again I was spared death, but no one questioned. No one dared, I suppose. I was the crown prince, the heir to the throne, the people's next monarch. Perhaps in their uneducated and blinded eyes, the gods had chosen to keep me safe, thereby grounding into themselves further the belief that my existence was preordained. I couldn't—shouldn't—die.

For their sakes.

And for their children's—and their children's children.

I suppose it was also preordained that I would begin to entertain suspicions when my seventeenth year came—the year when peculiar changes began to happen within me, and things to which I had never before given much thought suddenly grew in importance.

It was the year when I found myself inexplicably drawn toward a certain farmer's son, a temperamental, insufferable, and altogether splendid young man, whose family had been one of my father's favorite tenants. Leof. He'd been to court several times in the company of his father and brothers, but it wasn't till then when I began to notice things about him—little things that captured my fancy—little things that kept me awake at night, burdened with confusing thoughts and even more perplexing emotions.

To put it simply, he seduced me, in spite of the social chasm that separated us—and *especially* in spite of the questionable nature of our affair.

In fact, I allowed myself to be seduced, as it had always been what I wanted, and knowing that he returned my feelings justified the risks I took. When his name was drawn in the lottery, I was convinced that he was condemned by the gods for the loss of my innocence at his hands. I grieved, yes, when he was delivered to his death—and yet—*yet*—I couldn't help but listen to a quiet, nagging voice in the back of my mind. Things, it said, might not be as clear or as simple as they seemed.

I was quiet enough, not given to spontaneous conversation or ready mingling with others. That made it easy for me to spy on those close to me in spite of the treacherous nature of the whole thing. I waited and observed, withdrawing into inconspicuous corners and shadows until my presence was no longer felt (nor was it missed).

And from there, I began to notice hints—a word or two casually dropped between my father and one of his trusted aides—that alerted me to things that I'd never thought were possible.

Hints of a trust so readily betrayed, not so much between subjects and liege, but between father and son. Quiet reassurances from one man to another, whispered demands from king to servants.

"The crown prince is safe?"

"Yes, your Majesty."

I held my tongue as I strained my ears and sharpened my eyes. Disbelief and perhaps denial kept me from acting sooner. All the same, the day finally came for me to prove my suspicions and to lay my mind to rest.

It was the week before the next lottery.

Visiting diplomats had arrived, and the castle was kept busy. My father was hardly seen, and so were his ministers. I was charged by all to keep my distance for the time being and to immerse myself in my usual activities with which to pass the time. These diplomatic visits always portended idle hours on my part, being much too young and inexperienced (at least in their eyes) to be allowed for a moment in the company of foreign delegates.

So I explored.

Waiting for the right moment when all attention was fixed on the nurturing and development of diplomatic relations, I found my way to my father's private chambers. A door connected it to another smaller, more private room, and there the lottery chest was kept. It didn't prove too difficult to find a copy of the key. I had one in my possession, having come upon it by accident, when a careless servant had dropped it in his haste a few days before. I never surrendered it and kept it close in the expectation of finding some good use for it someday.

I entered the room and locked the door behind me, falling immediately to my knees before the chest. The pile of black wooden chips, on which was scrawled the names of every boy and girl between thirteen and twenty-one in crude, white letters, was intimidating.

Indeed, I began to doubt my instincts and rationalized what I could of the situation. The lots in the chest seemed thick and endless in spite of the fact that my kingdom had always been a tiny one, with the general population dwindling not so much because of the lottery, but because of other natural calamities. Ill health and disease were the most formidable forces that kept the population dangerously small.

All the same, I thought that it was most likely that the wooden chip bearing my name was lost in the collection and that for four straight years it had managed to keep out of the way of probing hands.

A gnawing desire to know the truth goaded me on, however, and I was soon digging my way through the lots.

The process was long and laborious. My arms ached, my back screamed for relief, and my head throbbed, but I refused to stop. I pulled out every one of those chips, reading the names to myself and searching desperately for mine.

It never materialized.

I reached the bottom of the chest and had plucked out the final lot—and my name remained missing. The truth of my fortune hit me between the eyes and made my stomach turn.

I was spared death because I was never part of the lottery in the first place. The chip bearing my name had never existed in spite of reassurances from both my father and his closest aides. Our people had been made into sniveling, wide-eyed dupes by the very people they thought worthy of their trust. I was made into a fool by my own father and the people I'd long considered friends and allies.

What devastated me the most was finding a sack hidden in another corner of the room—one that I thought contained the lots that bore the names of those who had died. I opened it and found that it contained wood chips, all bearing my deceased lover's name. My father and his aides had thought fit to punish him by ensuring his sacrifice in our most recent lottery by temporarily replacing the regular wood chips with those in the sack. Leof never had a chance.

Our illicit affair had been discovered. How and by whom, I didn't know, nor did I care to know at that moment.

I don't remember how long I sat there, raging tearfully and staring at the scattered pile of wood chips that surrounded me. I was pampered. Worthless. Made to look like an idiot before all those who knew me, without once lifting a finger to deserve it. Saved by the flouting of a law ordained by the very same man who found it in himself to dismiss it so easily without as much as a stirring in his conscience.

And I was saved from myself by the sacrifice of an innocent boy—one who'd done nothing more than open my eyes to my nature.

I thought of all those who died before me, most of whom I had known since childhood. I knew their parents and their families and even had the honor of being welcomed in their tiny, run-down cottages, eager to serve their next leader with whatever measly portions they could afford to spare. I'd become close friends with a handful and had wept at their deaths. Their faces were now forever seared in my memory, imprinted by the horrible deception I'd unmasked.

So I sat there, struggling to contain my rage and grief, lost in thought—then presently returned all the chips inside their container and left the room with my mind heavy with schemes and my heart swelling with the desire to right what had long been wrong.

The diplomats remained for a while, allowing me ample time to put my scheme into action. In the silence and the blackened cover of the night, I stole away from my room and ran out to the place where I knew my father had gotten the wood chips. That wasn't too difficult to do, the wood chips being nothing more than bits of bark chopped off trees that were destined for the hearth. I gathered all I could night after night, collecting them in my cloak and carrying them back to my room, where I went about the tedious task of sorting out the wood chips or breaking down the larger pieces in order to create a uniform enough collection.

Then I wrote my name on every single one of them.

I thought of every killed friend with every piece I labeled in white chalk.

Images of Bronwyn, Othilia, Alchfrith, Cyneric, Durwyn, and many others flooded my mind with every "Caedmon, son of Awiergan" I scrawled on the crumbling bark. With every piece I labeled, I felt one death avenged. With every piece I labeled, I saw less and less of my life beyond the coming week until nothing filled my brain but a dark, hollow void. And yet, I felt comforted.

I thought of Leof and the welcome opportunity of finding my way back to his side, where no one would ever have the means of separating us forever.

It took some doing, and it was not an easy task to accomplish, but when the time was right, I returned to my father's chambers and emptied out the chest, replacing all the lots with the ones I'd made, making sure to throw the original names into the fire I'd started in my room.

Then it was all a matter of waiting.

The diplomats left, heavy with food and wine, contented with cloying praises and empty promises heaped on their heads by those who knew best how to handle foreign relations. Treaties were signed, connections and alliances solidified, and yet for all these, not one could offer any means of relieving us of the dragon's plague, all of them being just as backward and superstitious and weak as my own kingdom. Or perhaps none of them wanted to extend their help. My father's ambitions lay in expansion, not in protection, after all, and he'd never hidden that fact. I suppose that explained a great deal of our vulnerability against forces such as the beast that haunted us.

The day of the lottery arrived, and as before, we all gathered before my father's castle, with the royal family standing proudly on the elevated platform and looking out with condescending pity at the huddled, soiled masses. The sky was gray and dull, the clouds that hung overhead serving as a thick, depressing canopy that didn't offer a break anywhere for the sun's light to shine through, no matter how faint. I could barely stifle a smile when the chest was opened, and one of my father's ministers stepped forward to do the honors.

He dug his hand inside, making a show of moving the lots about, mixing them up and perhaps thinking that he was somehow dictating people's chances of being chosen. I waited silently, my eyes fixed on my subjects and taking in the endless sea of weathered, care-worn faces. Every crease on their sunburned skin justified my deception, and I exulted for their sakes.

The minister pulled out a lot and stared at the name on it, falling silent for a moment.

"Well?" my father demanded. He sat in the middle of the platform, looking every bit the majestic, god-like figure he was made to be. "Who is it?"

The man seemed to tremble before everyone, raising his eyes and looking as though he preferred to be cut down with a sword right then and there instead of sharing what information he had. Another prodding from my father—one marked by growing irritation—loosened his tongue.

"Caedmon, son of Awiergan," he stammered.

Terrifying silence met the declaration. It was cold and numbing—lifeless. I half-expected myself to be sucked into the deafening void and so shifted a little nervously on my feet.

"Are you sure?" my father finally asked, his voice falling to a hoarse whisper. He'd turned pale—white, almost. His hands gripped the armrests, his knuckles standing in stark relief against his aging skin. I could tell that he was aching to leap to his feet, push the man aside, and tear through the lots himself. The shock and the desperation and disbelief that lit his eyes when our gazes met sent a terrible thrill of delight coursing through my veins. I returned the look with one of calm derision. I watched his eyes widen and realization slowly make itself known in the way he wordlessly moved his mouth in a vain attempt at expressing his shock. He understood that I'd discovered his duplicity, and there wasn't anything he could do to save me.

What was there, after all? The people would tear him to pieces, king or no king, if he were to demand another lottery. What justification would he have? What would he tell those who'd lost their children to the monthly sacrifice? Was it not his own edict that the crown prince would be on equal footing with all the other young people where the lottery was concerned? They would learn the truth—if not from him then from me. And they wouldn't be a happy, forgiving crowd.

Father and I stared at each other in silence for what seemed to be an eternity, neither of us flinching, our connection broken only when he finally spoke in a voice that trembled.

"The prince it is, then," he said, turning away to face his people and weakly drawing himself up with whatever pride was left in him.

I didn't receive the same displays of grief from my family. Nobility never allowed their emotions to show, after all. Whatever passions we felt were always subdued, suppressed into quieter, more dignified expressions of joy, anger, sadness, and terror. I turned to my mother and my sister and found them regarding me with perfectly controlled faces. For a brief moment I didn't even know if they truly felt anything for me, and I must admit to feeling a touch of resentment toward them and jealousy toward my poorer counterparts and their spontaneous bursts of emotion.

I could only bow before them and allow myself to be escorted away by shocked and reluctant guards.

Like my deceased predecessors, I was led to the tower room, where I was cleaned and dipped in aromatic water before being dressed as a bridegroom. Then I was led away.

There must have been a crowd that lined the streets where I was escorted. I don't remember now. Most likely. I honestly couldn't say what it was I saw or heard or felt during those moments of preparation. Things seemed to drift before my eyes as though in a dream—images and sounds and tactile sensations seemed distant and so far removed from the moment that I began to wonder if I were imagining the entire thing. I know that I must have moved mechanically and without thought as I was ushered here and there. I do remember not speaking a single word.

I was led to the boulder, and there I was chained. It wasn't the most comfortable position, as the monstrous piece of stone against which I was shackled leaned back a little so that I was almost resting against it, but the iron cuffs that were chained to the rock dangled above me so that I had my arms raised above my head, rendering me even more vulnerable to whatever might come my way. I couldn't imagine those poor girls, who were slighter of build and shorter than I—how they must have suffered through the discomfort of hanging down by their wrists. All I could say was that I was grateful that their deaths came swiftly and surely.

My escorts abandoned me with quiet words of regret and grief, which I tried to assuage with as much dignity I could muster at that moment. I offered them some comfort, charging them to look after my mother and my sister before blessing them and their families.

I was soon alone. The rock faced the edge of the cliff, where I understood the dragon made its appearance at a precise time of the day. The monster must have lived somewhere near the bottom of the canyon—perhaps inside the cliff walls. Nobody ever managed to discover that. I tried to find out for myself several times, but my father's patrols had caught me attempting to steal past the borders and brought me back to the castle, where I was admonished to keep to my place and where I spent the rest of the day being told what to do just to stay out of everyone's way.

As I waited, I rested my eyes on the panorama before me.

Just beyond the cliff's edge lay a vast expanse of land—untouched, rugged, majestic in its wildness. Distant mountains rose out of heavy mists as though to meet the sky, their jagged tips powdered with snow. Those rugged formations caught the sun's rays and reflected them in flashes of blinding light. The clouds had broken, allowing light to pierce through the gloom that defined the land. I counted myself blessed enough to be witness to the grandeur before me. The mountains seemed to stretch on forever, no matter where I looked, providing me with an odd sense of comfort at the thought of finality and permanence and infinity.

My friends had seen all this. Their final moment alive was spent in quiet contemplation of the stark silhouettes that spread before them. Their hearts were calmed by the gentle silence of the world around them. I was grateful for at least that point.

So I lost myself in my environment, closing my eyes to rest while I waited. I have no idea how long I stayed that way. It must have been several minutes or even hours. All I knew, all I understood, was being gently roused from my sleep and almost crying out from the pain of cramped and stretched muscles.

I opened my eyes and found myself staring at a knight.

A young one who seemed to be twenty-five years old—surprisingly young for a knight, I thought, but it could very well be nothing more than a reflection of my limited knowledge. He looked as though he'd just been through a recent battle or at least had been wandering the lands for some time. He held his helm against himself with one hand and a tall spear in another, and I saw that his armor was stained and dulled, dented in a few places and muddy in others. His hair, which was a pale shade of gold, was dulled with dust from his travels. Some strands, being moistened with sweat, clung to his skin in little gold-brown patches. His face was smeared with dust streaked with sweat. His cloak, along with his surcoat, were torn, faded, and soiled with dried mud. An equally stained and dulled broadsword hung on his left hip. Several feet away, under the shade of a small thicket, stood his horse—a majestic gray animal that seemed to radiate raw power with every small movement and twitch of its muscular form—also heavily soiled and looking rather grateful for the respite.

I stared at him in some surprise for several seconds.

"Who put you here?" he finally asked in a voice that spoke to me of a mind more inclined to quieter pursuits. I found the contrast jarring but not objectionable. It was—oddly fitting.

"My people did," I replied, shifting a little to ease the strain in my arms and listening to the chains clatter against the stone. "You can't stay here. It's too dangerous."

"Why did your people put you here? Are you being punished?"

"No, I..."

I had to pause and reconsider, my mind suddenly unraveling. In truth, after all, I was being punished. I was punishing myself for my friends' deaths. For my lover's execution. For my father's greed. So I simply stated a fact.

"I'm to be a sacrifice."

"To what?"

"A plague—a dragon."

He waited for a second or two, a picture of the utmost patience in spite of obvious signs of weariness. Looking down at me with eyes that defied his soiled features, he fixed me with a gaze of brilliant blue—reflecting a light of subdued curiosity and a hint of an older man's expectation. It felt as though he knew what I was about to say—as though he were simply listening to me confirm his suspicions, a habit, I suppose, that was created and shaped by time spent on the road, wandering far and wide.

I saw an older man's mind, heart, and spirit in a youth's body.

Returning his look and feeling that growing gulf between us in terms of experience, I began to feel insubstantial and ineffectual. Suddenly my purpose seemed foolish, selfish, and downright laughable.

In fact, I almost burst out laughing in complete contempt of myself—the pampered, sheltered, helpless prince, who, even on the verge of completing an act of sacrifice, was still as naïve and foolish as before, in spite of all prior convictions of justice and honor.

So I told my would-be rescuer about the dragon and its curse on my kingdom and my people's weakness and soldiers' ineffectiveness in defeating the menace. Of my father's final declaration of a law, when all seemed hopeless, that he was bound to break, a law that reflected the true weakness of those who'd long considered themselves a good deal wiser and better than their inferiors.

I told him everything—even of Leof.

I suppose I wished him to know of my unnatural propensities, hoping that he would feel outraged enough to leave me to my death.

My confession burdened me with an overwhelming sense of shame. My face warmed up in spite of the sudden rise of the winds around us.

Without speaking another word, he stepped forward and came up to me, studying me for a moment as though weighing my words before setting his weapon aside and reaching up to feel the shackles that encircled my wrists. The angled surface of the rock forced him to press himself lightly against me in order to reach the rusted rings of iron.

"You can't free me," I said, my words coming out in a choked half-whisper. He smelled of dirt and sun and sweat, the bitter, salty scent commingling with what I assumed to be his natural essence—a subtle, intoxicating musk of flesh somewhat heated by exertion.

It was Leof's smell. I recognized it, and I ached for it, the misery of our forced separation bursting out of its confines. I had to fight back the tears though I couldn't find it in myself to turn away—and sought solace by pressing my face subtly against his armored shoulder and inhaling deeply.

"These chains are old," he said. "A sword stroke would do it."

"Would it?"

"Yes. Your cuffs, though..." Here he tugged at the manacles. "We'll have to find a blacksmith who can work through the locks."

He stepped away and collected his weapon, and I found myself suddenly cold and exposed and, for a fleeting moment, utterly confused.

"You can't stay," I said, feeling a shift in the winds and blinking away the stray hair that whipped across my face as I spoke. I could sense something in the air. A stench rose with the winds' currents. "Unless you want to die, you can't stay here with me. Save your heroics for someone else."

The knight cocked his head, lifting a gloved hand to push wildly flailing strands of hair from his face. He cracked a slight, almost sympathetic smile.

"I'm bound by my oath to protect," he said, his voice barely heard in the swirling of air around us. I anxiously glanced around but found nothing amiss. "If it's justice you want, you won't find it in a monster's belly."

"This is stupidity on your part!" I hissed, tugging at my shackles and feeling the rusted iron scratch my skin. "Leave! Now!"

His smile broadened. "Stupidity? Oh, and *this* isn't?"

He pointed at my bound wrists. Then he paused, stiffening, as though listening for something. He nodded almost absently, stepping forward to lean his spear against the rock and placing his helm over his head, his eyes meeting mine just before they were obscured by the tarnished cylindrical cover. I thought I saw them sparkle cheerfully amid the shadows and the dirt.

"I'd be happy to engage you in a debate over who deserves what fate, Your Highness, but at the moment, my duty supersedes yours. Had you not been chained, I wouldn't dare overstep my bounds and defy you. Right now, however, you're at a rather *huge* disadvantage, and I'm better off ignoring questions or protests you might have."

Without waiting for a response, he hurried to his horse, untethered it, and let it run. Foolish, I thought, as he was now alone, unless by some luck his horse didn't wander too far. Then the knight was back, taking his place before me.

The winds picked up speed until it felt as though we were caught in the middle of a swirling funnel. I could barely keep my eyes open, while my hair and clothes whipped around me in a fury, threatening to tear themselves off my body.

The chains above me rattled as I felt my bound hands pulled and tugged against their constraints by the raging movement around me, the iron bands tearing at my skin, the roughness of the rock scraping my knuckles. Before me, the knight managed to keep his balance by digging his spear into the ground and bracing himself against it as he turned his back to me to face the yawning chasm.

The wind howled, and I thought that I was going to be driven mad from the frightful screeching. I cringed, unable to protect myself, before I realized that the howling that was tearing through my system wasn't that of the wind. Along with the swirling air that enveloped us, the frightful shrieking in the air grew more and more pronounced until it was clear to my shattered senses that the noises came from the belly of the very beast that had now come to claim me.

I managed to crack open my eyes in time to catch sight of the knight standing before me, his cloak and surcoat flapping wildly as he braced himself against the winds. He didn't move away from his position, his figure looking much too small and fragile against the landscape that scowled at him from a distance. And for the briefest moment, I felt an overwhelming sense of protectiveness toward him as a voice started to scream from the back of my mind, urging me to pull him back and take him far, far away from that dreadful place.

*He's too young*, it hissed in my ears. *He'll die because of you.*

"No," I gasped, tugging at the chains that held me fast. "I couldn't help it—it's not my fault—I didn't ask him to come!"

The winds picked up for yet another second before the cursed monster appeared, flying into view from the canyon below. The knight before me staggered back a few steps in surprise at the sudden apparition. I watched, horrified, at the beast as it hovered above, looking down on us with bulging yellow eyes, its pupils nothing more than angry black slits that sliced down the center of each eyeball. Its scales glinted in the sun in discordant flashes of green and yellow, the texture both smooth and roughened, its claws curling into savage arcs with deadly, sharp points. Its wings stretched out from side to side like monstrous bats' wings of gold and green, flapping awkwardly because of their sheer size.

*He'll die because of you!* the voice insisted.

"No!" I cried out, and the monster opened its jaws, baring its teeth and snake-like tongue, and let loose another unnatural scream that froze my blood. "I didn't ask him to come!"

The knight—as though nothing awful were happening—strode casually forward, gripping his spear with both hands as he watched his nemesis hover before him, howling its rage, slime dripping from its jaws. The man looked too small. Too small. He wasn't even armed properly. The whole thing seemed absurd. And yet there he was, facing certain death with all the air of superiority that perhaps any warrior, who was ridiculously sure of himself, possessed.

A torrent of curses poured out of my mouth as I jerked and tugged violently at my shackles. "Don't do this!" I cried out, my voice sounding too thin and vague in my ears.

*It's your fault.*

"No! I didn't know that he'd come! It's not..."

*Your fault.*

"No! I didn't ask him to save me! I didn't ask him to..."

*And neither did your friends—did they?*

I paused, blinking away the tears that had gathered. The dragon flapped its scaly wings, lifting itself up higher, its eyes still fixed on the knight in front of me.

*Your friends and Leof—they didn't ask you to come. They didn't ask you to save them.*

The monster screeched one more time before hurtling back down, shooting through the air like a massive, repulsive arrow that glinted in the sun. It opened its jaws and bared its teeth, and red fire issued from its throat, leaving a trail of gray mist behind. The knight paused and waited near the edge of the cliff.

*You couldn't help what had happened to them. It's not your burden to bear.*

"My father killed them," I whispered.

*It was chance and chance alone. What guarantee did you have of being chosen had your lot been there since the beginning? Would you still sacrifice yourself for them if your name hadn't been pulled?*

"Then what of Leof?"

*That—I cannot say.*

"I'm justified then."

A loud, guttural hiss. The dragon roared as it tried to snap its jaws on the vulnerable figure that awaited it by the cliff's edge. The knight braced himself and waited for the right moment.

I held my breath then involuntarily cried, "The heart! Strike at the heart!" when I realized that he seemed to be aiming at a part of the monster that wouldn't guarantee an easier battle. I remained unheeded, however.

Gripping the spear securely in both hands, he heaved and drove the spear's point into the monster's mouth, burying it deeply inside its throat. A scream of pain followed, and I thought I felt the ground beneath me tremble as it snapped its head back, howling in pain, its jaws wide open. The knight had let go of his weapon, leaving it embedded inside the monster's throat and watching it disintegrate as it was consumed by bright red fire that continued to issue forth. He stumbled back as a wing beat against him, knocking him down while the beast reared up and thrashed about in mid-air, shaking its head sharply in an effort to dislodge the burning spear.

I was aghast. "Fool," I hissed. "How would that help?" A spear. He had attacked with a weak, ineffectual weapon against a force that was too great for him.

The knight lost no time. Even after landing hard on his back, he still managed to roll himself over and stagger to his feet, unsheathing his sword (the only weapon left to him) as he struggled to pull himself upright. I could tell, with a painfully constricting heart, that he was exhausted, his armor weighing him down. I was furious at myself and my helplessness.

*Will your sacrifice bring them back?*

"No," I whispered brokenly, slumping against the rock as I watched the battle with an anxiety that crippled me. "Nothing will."

*Will your death stop this monster?*

"No."

*Then let him avenge in your name.*

I could only fall silent and struggle to subdue the wild pounding of my heart. My eyes were inexorably fixed on the knight's soiled and metallic figure ahead, misty with unshed tears of anger and shame.

I watched him grip his soiled and dented sword with both hands, his body taut and trembling from the extremity of the tension—as though tightly coiled to the point of shattering itself. It wouldn't take much for that coil to release itself in one massive explosion of power.

A faint shower of ash flew out of the dragon's mouth as the spear was completely consumed. It once again threw its head back, letting forth another terrible cry that filled the chasm before rising up for leverage and then flying back down, still screaming its rage and pain. I did notice, however, that no fire issued out of its jaws now. Having been injured in the very place where the flames formed, it had been crippled and made more vulnerable against the knight's attacks.

I stared on in amazement. The knight—that filthy, travel-weary, and foolish youth—took advantage of his *disadvantage* against the monster and won himself a greater chance at victory.

The monster dove down, whipping its head forward as though it were at the end of a lash, opening its injured jaws wide open. The knight waited for the precise moment when slime-covered and bloodied teeth reached out for him, then he suddenly dove down and rolled with an agility that astonished me until he was under the beast's body. He swung his sword in a wide, desperate arc, cutting a large gash on the scale-covered juncture where the monster's neck and chest met. I could even hear the sickening sound of blade tearing through scale and skin.

The dragon, taken aback by the sudden move, roared once again, but the time it crashed on the ground before me, writhing in pain while blood began to flow from the new wound. It hadn't expected this resistance. For four full years, it had never once encountered a determined effort at thwarting its desires. It had clearly grown complacent and allowed its defenses to stagnate.

I couldn't help but smile as I watched it thrash about, screaming.

"That, you demon, was for Eadwyn." My mind flooded with memories of a boy—the son of my father's own groom and a close friend in my childhood—smaller and weaker than me and who, at fourteen, had been offered as a sacrifice to this detestable thing.

The knight had lost his sword when he scrambled out of the beast's way as it crashed on the cliff's edge, and he had to run several yards to reclaim it. The dragon paused, momentarily distracted from its injuries. The knight stumbled away, burdened by the awkward armor he wore, and the dragon sniffed after him. It would catch him before he even reached his weapon.

"Here!" I screamed, rattling the chains. "Here!"

The monster turned its head. Its eyes settled on me, and it growled.

"I'm here! Come and take me!"

It snarled, shaking its head a little, before raising itself up to slither toward me. A dank, repulsive trail formed as it moved, and I felt my stomach turn from the rising stench of slime and blood. I forced myself to meet its furious, hateful stare as low rumblings gurgled from its bleeding throat. It stopped before me, distracted by the possibility of an easy meal. Its jaws were a few feet away, and as it smelled me, I could feel the moist heat that came out of its nostrils. I steeled myself against its looming, terrifying form and hoped that the knight had reached his sword safely.

And in a grotesque parody of a dog eager to find favor in its beloved master's hands, the dragon alternately growled and hissed as its tongue snaked out, running its wet, forked tip up and down my body, covering me with its disgusting fluid. I couldn't suppress a small moan of revulsion as I turned my head when its rough surface scraped up my chest to my neck. I shivered from the contact and vainly pressed myself against the rock on my back. The monster continued its exploration as its tongue shifted direction and slid down my body, and I was shaking from the stifled urge to cry out in protest, but my need to offer myself in such a degrading, repugnant fashion overrode all natural responses.

I turned, sickened, just when the monster retracted its tongue and began to open its jaws. I saw the teeth that had torn my friends and peers into ribbons. I saw, for the briefest, most fleeting moment, the ghastly throat that had swallowed Leof. Then all semblance of control left me, and I screamed my rage.

The dragon suddenly reared up, shrieking at the sky, and for a second I thought that it was somehow mimicking me. But it violently turned, its wings pulling up with a jerk, though it didn't attempt to fly.

A small figure bolted before me, running with sword in hand from one side of the monster to the other, raising its weapon high just as the wings came down and slashing a large, jagged tear across the leathery skin. I then realized that the other wing had been similarly disabled. This was the knight's offensive maneuver that had pulled the beast so quickly and so unexpectedly away from me.

The dragon's howls rose higher in both tone and pitch. It couldn't escape now.

"For Elwine and for Willan," I managed to say.

It was now a battle between equals, and I watched, with horrified and insane fascination the massive injured bulk of green and gold monstrosity let loose its rage on its smaller opponent. It reared and lunged clumsily now. The knight leaped and ran, jumped and rolled, exerting every ounce of whatever available energy he had left to confuse, jar, and cripple his opponent. Every now and then he would swing his sword and cut another wound at another part of the monster's body, and I saw that he was still aiming for those that afforded the dragon any sense of mobility. The legs and the shoulders as well as the hips were stabbed and cut, allowing him plenty of time to be on the defensive as he continued to tire out the creature.

He would take the occasional blow of an awkwardly swung limb or wing, but his determination offered him the push to recover in spite of his increasing slowness. The fatigue was great.

I felt my spirit merge with his, and with every bloody stroke of the sword, it was as though I myself were doing it. And so I reveled in the fight. Primitive responses to my rage and the rage that goaded both combatants on infused me with a terrible frenzy that I'd never before known, and I was trembling in my shackles as I spat out name after name of every victim with each hissing of the sword.

Alodia, daughter of Wallace.

A stab in the flank.

Synne, daughter of Bestandan.

A cut across the shoulder.

Boniface, son of Fugol.

A slice at the jaw.

Aglaeca, son of Yrre.

The dragon continued to fight, snapping its jaws and roaring at the winds. It rolled, thrashed, writhed, lunged, and slithered, its movements growing clumsier and more distracted. And after what seemed like an eternity, it received another mortal wound on its chest, and it threw its head back, gurgling its fury. The knight immediately pulled his sword out and stumbled wearily back a few paces, setting himself before his enemy just so, then he shifted the sword in his hands and raised his arms, holding the weapon as though it were a massive dagger. He was panting and gasping from his exertions, and it seemed that he barely had the strength left to deliver the final blow.

With a loud cry, he stumbled forward and threw himself against the beast, using his entire body as he buried his sword in the beast's heart, pushing and pushing until only the hilt was left, and he was pressed against the blood-soaked scales.

Time stopped. I watched as they remained fixed where they stood, with the monster partly reared up, the knight against its chest in a bizarre attitude of a loving embrace. Then it was over.

The monster struggled one final time, lifting itself up with tattered wings and allowing the knight to pull his sword out of its body before it rolled over and fell off the edge of the cliff, its death cries filling the chasm and fading off in the distance.

The silence that followed descended on us heavily, and neither of us moved for several seconds. I listened, with numbed senses, as the wind once again rose up around us, purging the bloodstained air of its hideous elements.

I watched the champion fall to his knees, dropping his ruined sword to the ground. There he stayed with his head bowed and his body heaving with weary gasps, all his weight being held up by mail-covered hands that trembled on the grass beneath him. I leaned against the rock, feeling complete exhaustion overpower me. I was sweating, and the wetness lavished on me by that vile tongue made my clothes cling to my body, cooling my skin and making me shudder from disgust at the sensation and the stench that began to rise up with every blow of the wind.

I closed my eyes and offered silent prayers to my friends. I blessed my people and my family.

With eyes newly opened to bitter truths, I felt at a loss, unable to decide whether or not I ought to return. The obligation that faced me as the next king oppressed my shaken spirits. There was so much change that needed to be made. The effects of so many years of ineffective leadership needed to be purged, the people's faith and confidence in their own abilities to govern their lives under better rules, restored. How would I face my father? With his chosen ministers and aides no better than he, how would I expect to bring about the changes necessary for the kingdom to prosper the way that it should?

I heard the sudden clanging of steel against stone, and my arms, so lately cramped in their awkward position above my head, fell to my sides. I opened my eyes to find myself staring up at the conqueror, who had now taken off his helm to expose his youthful, muddied, and bruised countenance to my gaze. He smiled wanly, his eyes still bright amid all the darker reminders of his oaths as a protector of the oppressed. I saw that his sword was badly damaged and useless.

I felt myself irrevocably bound to him. I owed him much more than I could ever express. For all my shortcomings and frailties, I swore then that I would, in my turn, be his protector. He seemed to have read my thoughts as his smile broadened a little, an air of embarrassment suddenly on him.

"It's my duty to serve," he said. Those were the only words that passed between us at that moment, and I didn't think that we needed any more. I stepped forward and wrapped my arms around him in a tight, relieved embrace. I felt him slump wearily against me, and I gratefully accepted the burden of his weight. I held him up and silently urged him to place himself in my hands, and I think that he understood me well enough.

Memories of my final moments with Leof trickled through my mind. I had held him in very much the same way, offering what little strength I had to assure him of my devotion to him. Leof told me, in his own unpolished way, to move on and look elsewhere for my happiness, and I was soon the one being held up in turn, broken against his shoulder. The condemned would be the one to offer me comfort instead. It was with a good deal of shame that I looked back at that moment.

All that would be left of Leof would be a ring that his father had given to him when he was set to take over their farm. He had no one left in his family, his older brothers dying from illnesses, so I asked to keep it safe. It had remained my most valuable possession ever since.

I don't remember how long the champion and I stood there, holding each other tightly, ignoring all rules of decorum or those that separated ranks and dictated our set places in the tapestry that wove us all together. Call it arrogance, call it a foolish presumption—but at that moment, I never believed any of those cursed rules applied to us.

It had been a dozen years since.

My kingdom is small still, but it's prospering nicely. On taking over my father's place, I had turned everything upside-down, discarding forty-odd years of his rule and struggling to rebuild my people's lives. We've temporarily cut ourselves from the outside world and have bent all our thoughts on building up our wealth and security. It was difficult, and several times in the course of my rule I felt the painful, overwhelming desire to give up, but I was bound by my duty to my people—to my long-lost friends—and to Leof. I suppose it was really for their sakes that I had worked myself to the point of collapse. I felt it a small compensation, given the enormity of their loss, but I suppose it would have to do.

Elne thought it so. He's still my protector, and I his. He has helped me through the long, arduous years of change and has grown to be my closest, most trusted aide.

My best friend.

My fiercest ally.

My greatest advisor.

I've also since then found warmth in the arms of another—a nobleman whose identity will remain hidden and whose company I'll forever seek in the cover of darkness. A change of laws, after all, doesn't guarantee the defeat of prejudices. I'm not afraid, nor am I displeased with our forced secrecy. As in all things, one can't have everything worth having. At the very least we have Elne's unconditional devotion to our shield.

Several times in the course of my rule, I silently blessed the day when chance dictated the direction of this knight's steps and human nature for my impetuous, foolish whims.

I still do.

The horse galloped into the midnight fog. Throughout the ride, Baltasar couldn't see much more than the mad light in the animal's eyes, the distorted grimace that pulled the mouth wide open, the square teeth exposed to the moon, the flaring of nostrils giving out bursts of smoky exhalations into the chill night. Its brown body heaved with violence, and Baltasar's hold on the reins tightened.

"God help me," he prayed fiercely. "God help me."

In his mind's eye he saw his father waiting for him at the end of the dark road, standing firm and tall before their family's cottage, his fury spiraling with every passing minute. *You belong here. Nowhere else. You owe us much, and you will* not *shirk your duties so easily.*

Baltasar could hear those words in his head, repeated with every thundering hoof beat. Familiar words, really, having been spoken far too many times by his father, his mother, and an uncle. Those same words had been ground into his older brothers and sisters, who'd long moved on to marry and raise children without a word raised in complaint, not a single second of hesitation in their acquiescence. But Baltasar saw the shadows that haunted their eyes, the hollowness brought on by the continued and methodical squelching of a young person's will and independence. Whether or not his brothers and sisters truly enjoyed living the way they were living now, Baltasar couldn't rightly say, for they'd also grown very good in speaking as their parents had taught them to speak. He didn't know whether or not to trust what came out of their mouths, even in good will.

His body screamed from the strain of the ride. Flesh, bone, and sinew had been turned into a mass of tightly-coiled tension, his legs locked against the horse's flanks with cement-like stiffness. Why was he so desperate to take his place by his father's side again? Was it safety? Normalcy? Familiarity? The appeal of the predictable?

"I won't let you lose me, Papa. I *won't.*"

"And why should I lose *you?*" came the inevitable question.

The voice, disembodied, cracked with a pain for which, Baltasar knew, he and *only* he was responsible. The voice also seeped into his mind, fighting to retain an open channel between them. With Baltasar's frantic efforts at escape, taking a firm hold of his mind was all the pursuer could do, and words laced with bitterness and rejection trickled through in a relentless stream. Guilt swelled in Baltasar's heart under the words of recrimination, haunting him since the start of the chase. They lanced him again and again with reminders of what had been, of what *should* have been, though he insisted on denying it all. For his family's sake, of course, for he owed him much—no less than his life, in fact, as his father and mother often claimed, their voices always edged with a sternness that challenged him to disobey them.

He glanced over his shoulder and glimpsed his pursuer: once lover, now outcast villain. It was what had always been expected—indeed, demanded—of him.

*You've had your chance to test the waters. You've tasted what was forbidden, what was going to kill your soul and leave you friendless. We'll excuse your idiocy as long as you take your place with us again.* Those words, again crowding in his mind, fighting with the corresponding images of his father pacing angrily before their cottage, waiting for his youngest child to return with his pride checked, his head bowed, his tears ready to fall as he begged for his family's forgiveness.

Baltasar's gaze fell on the bright, leafy eyes of the Erl-king, who rode his feather-covered stallion with equal desperation nearly a dozen feet behind. His gaze was fixed on Baltasar. Not once did he mind the foggy road before them. He looked placid and confident, his complexion untouched by his exertions, berry lips curled in the barest hint of a smile. But when he reached out for his quarry, his fingers trembled, and his white palm glimmered with sweat. Suddenly, that calm confidence and phantom smile spoke of a violently suppressed longing and a deeply felt hurt that might not ever heal. Betrayals, after all, tended to wound beyond saving. Even immortals—perhaps *because* of their hopelessly eternal state—fell victim to them. Loneliness defined infinity, and the relief that was always sought was of the kind that would never come. Even at that distance, even in the dark, Baltasar could still see everything so clearly, perhaps because the Erl-King wished him to. Or was it his own heart?

Baltasar's conscience stung him again. As before, he struggled against it, determined to justify his ill choices with every scrap of rationalized thought he could dredge up in his fear.

That the Erl-king would want him puzzled him—or he *believed* it puzzled him. As a boy, and even now as a young man of seventeen, he wasn't much to see. His mind filled with memories of his childhood and early adolescence, and he winced at the reminders of protruding bone against colorless flesh. Of an awkward transition from childhood to youth, a transition that often left him friendless and alone, consigned to aimless wanderings in a lonely bid for solace.

*The Erl-king rides close, son. Beware of his influence. Never let him inside your mind. Can't you see him?*

"That's only the mist you see, Papa," Baltasar replied with forced calm. "It isn't him." For several desperate moments, Baltasar kept up a one-sided conversation with his parents, reassuring them under his breath that the Erl-king was nowhere near, that he was quite safe and on his way home, ready to throw himself at their feet and their mercy.

His grip on the reins tightened as he spurred his horse onward. Fly, his mind screamed, fly quickly! Far, far away, yes, from what his father always believed to be the all-too-real danger that came from dark magic as well as the bitter reminders of Baltasar's own willing forays into that fantastic world. The pain that ate away at his heart felt like poison that burned its way through his body.

Superstition had shaped his birth. Superstition defined his youth. Superstition, now, dictated the course of his future.

He heard the Erl-king call out his name, and he glanced back. His pursuer rode with greater urgency, the Erl-king's smooth brow lightly creased as he watched his human lover. Even in the shadow of the night, he shimmered in colors of which men could only dream, the mortal world being hued with not much more than gray, brown, and white.

The Erl-king's hair blew in thick waves of autumn, barely contained by a thin band of gold that sat proudly on his head. The crown spoke of his lineage and the honor which he'd been paying Baltasar, even now when he was chasing the terrified boy through the midnight fog. His clothes, all made from leaves, bark, and water, shifted in their shades and dazzled one's eyes with a kaleidoscope of November colors. With every thundering hoof beat, a handful of leaves would fly off into the darkness beyond, or bits of bark would flutter in his wake, or faint drops of water would shower the bleakness around them.

The Erl-king reached out for Baltasar again, and his fingers—*again*—fell far short of their mark. A spray of water, however, touched Baltasar's cheek, and the wetness trickling down his cold skin felt like tears though they might not be his.

*He's trying to speak to you, son! Don't listen! He means death, and you know it!*

"It's only your imagination, Papa. What you're hearing is the wind blowing through the trees." His cheeks felt icy and damp, and the way the scene before him seemed to lose its solid form, with details melting into each other as though viewed under water, convinced Baltasar it wasn't water from the Erl-king's person that drenched his face. It was tears.

As though in answer, the horse neighed madly, and, drawing sudden strength from its release, it plunged headlong into the darkness with fiercer speed.

"Why are you denying me? What have I done wrong?" the voice asked.

Baltasar could only shake his head, sobbing, and old memories were dragged out, forcing him to confront his past.

• • • •

MEMORIES OF HIS CHILDHOOD, of his being raised in a bubble of gray asceticism and a colorless calm. His eyes had been carefully shielded, his attention fixed on what was defined as true and good by his elders. He felt content all in all, as content as one would be, that is, having been given only *one* world of experience and nothing with which to compare it. Friends, of whom he'd had wretchedly few, dismissed him for a simpleton, for he'd been unable to keep up with their worldlier and more sophisticated ways.

His forced isolation made him turn to occasional rambles into the wilderness. He took paths that led him far from his home and all things comfortably familiar. He explored as only a young, hungry mind would explore. The years of saintly denial gnawed through his mind and, sadly for his well-meaning parents, allowed the boy to see the world through the tatters, enticing him to delve further.

Then, at sixteen, he began to listen to the grass. It really wasn't more than idle play, an effort at wasting precious time. At the point where consciousness and sleep met, he heard music—a voice singing. It was soft at first, tentative notes coaxed out of the leaves and the reeds, then it grew louder once he caught hold of it. The boy pressed his ear more firmly against the earth and listened with greater fervency.

Suddenly his mind was invaded by color: subtle hues at first, variations of black, white, and brown, followed by more complex shades, most of which he'd never seen. The slight trickling grew to a more energetic torrent of reds, blues, and yellows, and, overcome by the discordance, he lost consciousness.

There were tales of old that spoke of enchantment being broken by a lover's kiss. Not once, however, had he heard of charms being cast by one. But he found himself in such a story, when he awoke to the gentle pressure of a leafy kiss against his lips, and he saw a strange young king—a remarkable otherworldly nobleman who appeared to be of the same age as he—bending over him. The creature watched the boy closely with eyes as deep and lush as the wood, hair as vibrant as the fall, skin as clear as the brook. Baltasar was nearly blinded by the stranger's world.

"You look odd," he blurted out, his fingers feeling his mouth as he sat up drowsily. "Are you from the village?"

The young king smiled. "You've much to learn," he said, and those were the first notes of music Baltasar had ever heard. They were lullaby-like in their gentleness, laced with the loneliness of infinity. The creature called himself the Erl-king, the forest spirit.

"Are there others like you?" Baltasar frowned as he swept his gaze up and down the Erl-king's robes. He reached out a hand and tentatively touched a part of the hem and wondered at the material's softness and warmth—something so different from the coarse wool and linen with which he'd long been used.

"No. I live alone." The Erl-king smiled, but it was an empty one, and Baltasar knew exactly what he felt. "What's your name?"

"Baltasar."

"That's a pretty interesting name. I'm guessing it has a special meaning to your parents."

Baltasar shrugged. "It means 'protected by God.'"

"And are you?"

It took him a moment to think of his reply. "I can't rightly say, and I don't really think I want to be." The Erl-king laughed at hearing that, and Baltasar couldn't help but smile in turn.

So their connection began: isolated young king and friendless boy, immortal and human, teacher and pupil. Baltasar's wanderings took on a wholly different meaning, and he looked forward to them day after day. It was a frightening and altogether wonderful adventure for him to leave the gray solemnity and strictness of his home and then plunge headlong into a wild, untamed world of stark and blinding beauty. In the wood the two would walk, deep in conversation.

Several weeks passed till the inevitable moment came, when things took a different turn, one which left Baltasar with unfamiliar choices. It was inevitable, he believed, given the nature of his connection with the strange king.

"I want to see more," he said one day as he lay on the grass, awash in the spring sunlight. His teacher obliged him.

An immortal hand pressed against his chest, and Baltasar's clothes shivered under the pale touch. They dissolved and fluttered in bits off the boy's body, to be carried off by the breeze in a swirl of leaves, and Baltasar was left lying naked in the king's hold. He heard the call of birds and the singing of the streams, the feathered touch of the afternoon breeze and the taste of flowers. Those sensations seemed to stretch on and on, alternately fading and growing more vivid, each scent, sight, sound, touch, and taste of Nature in its alternate magical state working in tandem with the slow and gentle shedding of Baltasar's childhood and the inevitable awareness of what had been lost as well as what now lay awaiting him.

Their breathing calmed. With it came the lifting of enchanted mist, and all was once again clear and sharply defined. Baltasar lay on the grass, damp with dew and staring, suddenly horrified, at the figure that held him fast against itself.

The colors had grown too bright and too vivid. The sounds had become too discordant and grating in his ears. The texture of earth and flesh had grown harsh and painful. Gone were the safety and the harsh strictness of his father's world. Gone was the silence that comforted him.

Compounding his confusion and horror was his sudden shocking awareness of his lover's body. Beyond the magical strangeness of the Erl-king's clothes, there really wasn't anything different about his physicality. The Erl-king, in fact, seemed to mirror Baltasar in every sense: pale skin untouched by hours spent in the sun doing hard labor; a musculature that spoke volumes about the youth's age, with lean muscles and slightly protruding bones here and there; long and somewhat awkward limbs that promised strength in maturity. Yet Baltasar couldn't help but shrink under a sudden wave of embarrassment, shock, and painful self-consciousness.

The Erl-king remained silent the whole time, his bright eyes fixed on Baltasar, keen and sharp. He seemed to read the swell of confusion in Baltasar's mind and preferred to wait things out, though it was also clear that a shadow of doubt and even pain had clouded his features.

"We shouldn't have done that," Baltasar stammered, blanching. "It was wrong." Though he tried hard not to think about it, he could still see the looks on his parents' faces if they were to find out about this. He could even hear their voices in his head—the furious, bitter accusations and blame, the insinuations of his being a loose, unprincipled, immoral brat. Would they claim that he was trying to kill them as well? Yes, they would; it was easy to see and hear them. Would they demand his penance, demand a radical change in his perceptions regarding the true course of a young boy's maturation?

Discipline, a mind and heart clear of impure influences, and a readiness to sacrifice one's selfish will in favor of his family's greater good. Those would be his father's words, which would likely be echoed by his mother unless she were to break down in tears and impress upon him just how much hurt he'd caused her. *How could you be so selfish?*

"I never led you to do it," came the startled answer, "and you didn't seem to care one way or the other. Why does it matter now?"

Dichotomies Baltasar had long accepted as the way of the world—so easy and so comfortable and so, so familiar—were suddenly splintered into a vast, unpredictable scale of subtleties, incongruence, and contradictions *within* similarities. His childhood was nothing more than an easy-to-follow road paved in black and white, right and wrong. In one afternoon, those dichotomies melted into dozens of shades of gray that baffled and frightened and turned the world into a mess of uncertainty. Baltasar didn't know his mind all of a sudden, and he blamed the Erl-king for his inexplicable preference for another man's touch.

"I wish we never met," he said bitterly, and he sat up, blinking away the tears. "This is all your fault. I don't know how I'll be able to face my parents again."

"How easy it is for you to forget that I've lost something of myself to you as well," the Erl-king retorted as he sat up. He didn't reach out to comfort Baltasar despite the clear look on the immortal's face that said that he desperately needed to.

And how easy it was for Baltasar to be seduced by those words in spite of his shock, his older self now realized with a pang of shame. How easy it was for him at sixteen and then seventeen to fall into the comfort of an enchanted lover's arms, blurting out promises of love that seemed harmless and inconsequential in a fog of youthful naïveté. The allure of rebellion, perhaps, directed his steps forward, but it now seemed so foolish. So *foolish*. Because his family said so, and remnants of his childhood self reminded him that his parents always knew best.

It wouldn't be long for the day to come when the boy, now a young man despite the one-year jump in age, would emerge from his sensual languor to realize he was once again dogged by a familiar yet an unwelcome sensation: shame. How could he allow himself to be so easily led down the path of unnatural pleasure? Duty also called with a stronger and more insistent voice. At seventeen he pushed himself away from the Erl-king's embrace, the loss of his second innocence (as he'd called it) much greater and more excruciating to feel.

*You've done enough damage to your soul. Come back to us if you want to be cleansed. You've a lifetime to prepare for—adulthood, fatherhood, and by the grace of God, old age, with your grandchildren and great-grandchildren surrounding you with love and happiness. What guarantee of any of those do you have in his company? What guarantee of happiness can you expect from a demon?*

Baltasar fled without another look back. In this state he returned to the normalcy of mortal existence, hoping that the ascetic grayness of his former life would cloak his degradation in its predictable shadows and lead him to a better path ahead. He didn't want the vivid colors, the sharp scents, the exhilarating touch of the wind. There wasn't any room in his life for those—or for anything that led him away from the narrow and unyielding path that had long been meant for him. Besides, he'd already stayed outside well beyond his normal hours, and heaven only knew what awaited him on his return home. He dared not think about it, but he couldn't help himself from toying with possibility after possibility of physical punishment, and the more he did so, the more real it felt.

For the next several weeks he closed his eyes against the colors of the wood. He shut his ears from the melancholy voice that called for him among the trees. He stayed away from the wood and its immortal occupant, turning his mind back to those old and oft-repeated lessons, taking care to keep his gaze down in a show of humility and penance till his parents beamed with pride as they started to groom their youngest son for his entry into the world of adult men. For all his efforts, however, Baltasar's spirits remained low, for the voice in the wood never faded. He could even hear it in his sleep.

"And what the Devil's wrong with you now?" his father demanded one day.

Baltasar worked in the open market with his father. It was a role that was inevitable, one that he'd taken on after he turned seventeen. They sold only a few items, for their purpose was to exhibit his father's skills in woodcraft, and from there interested customers would hire the older man for specific commissions. Business had been good, with requests coming in from nearby towns and villages in Bremen. However, Baltasar remained distracted and uninterested in the goings-on around him, and he went through his day silently taking people's money and wrapping up wooden toys or household ornaments.

"Nothing, Papa," Baltasar replied. "I'm just doing my job."

"If you were really doing your job, you'd have realized that you overcharged this woman and gave the wrong change to at least four people. What's the matter? Are you sick?"

"I'm not, I swear!"

Baltasar was never a good liar; for that his parents should be pleased, for it was their teaching that ingrained it in him. But it was also a dangerous quality, as the boy was about to discover. There was simply no way around it.

On their way home from the market, Baltasar's father pulled the wagon aside, and in the twilight hours and the deepening shadows of the wood's borders, he beat the truth out of his son. Under the sharp, painful strokes of a slender wooden rod, Baltasar mixed a halting confession with pleas for mercy, his cries of pain echoing through the wood, his father's grunts of disgust, disappointment, and rage slicing through his mind.

The boy didn't know how long it took for his father to satisfy himself with his confession, but the unspeakable pain that wracked his body and the terrible grief caused by his father's curses convinced him it must have been an eternity. Once the final stroke was done, Baltasar found himself crumpled on the ground, his body nothing more than a mass of pain. His father didn't aim for a specific body part in his rage; the rod whistled countless times in terrifying succession, on random areas all over, save for his head, and now everything sang in agony.

"I'm leaving you one of the horses," his father ground out between tightly clenched teeth. "Get yourself back together and come back home before the hour's up, or by God, you'll regret your obstinacy. You'll not upset your mother with your blubbing, do you understand me?"

Baltasar could only wait, crying and listening to the sounds of one of the horses being released from the wagon, prepared for riding, and then tethered to a nearby tree.

"One hour, Baltasar." And with that, his father was gone.

The boy exhausted himself in his grief, and he forced himself to move presently. It had already grown dark, with nothing but the moon's light showing the way back to his parents' cottage. It had been well over an hour already.

"Baltasar?"

He drew a sleeve across his eyes and blinked away the tears, turning to find the Erl-king standing in the shadows, watching and waiting. The Erl-king glowed in the dark, allowing Baltasar to see him more easily and read what he could of his lover's thoughts and feelings. The magical youth stood tall and erect, proud and untouchable despite his cursed existence of eternal loneliness. Baltasar could see pain shadowed in his lover's eyes, most likely because of his denial of their bond, but all those years spent in isolation and yearning had also hardened the woodland spirit to a point. He could sense caution and doubt in the midst of heartbreak.

"I'll be all right," Baltasar replied, his voice hoarse and nasal. He could barely breathe, and his eyes were swollen. "Papa was right. I owe him and Mama my life. The least I could do is be the son they always wanted."

The Erl-king frowned a little but said nothing. Baltasar knew he didn't believe him, for his own words rang hollow even to himself. He stumbled over to the horse, wincing from the pain with every faltering step he took.

"That isn't who you are."

"I rebelled. That's all." Baltasar spared the Erl-king a glance. "It meant nothing to me."

He mounted the horse, gritting his teeth with every stab of pain that coursed through him, taking care not to look in the Erl-king's direction again for fear of seeing the other youth's reaction to his dismissal. He didn't want to see it, for he knew it would only convince him to stay, to be a permanent part of the open world and its ever-changing landscape—of meadows and mountains, lakes and forests, blue skies and dark oceans. The possibilities were frightening, certainly not even worth considering.

Baltasar knew the discordance of color was preferable to the calm of grays, and the crude beauty of woodland music was a balm to his deafened ears. There was comfort in the predictability and serenity his family offered, but in that solace was a crippling stagnation of which he was now painfully aware. All the same, he wished for it, having now tasted its maddening counterpart.

"No," he'd ground out as he urged his horse on. "None of that's normal. *None.*" Oh, yes, he sounded very much like the kind of son who'd make his parents proud.

• • • •

HE CAST ONE FINAL GLANCE over his shoulder and gauged his spurned lover's progress. The Erl-king now regarded him with unmistakable anger, though he still reached out for Baltasar, a desperate attempt at offering him a final chance, which he once again shrugged off. The pale hand that sought him out in the dark grew fainter and fainter, and he took heart in this, shouting at his horse to run, run from the Devil.

*Son, I see others in the shadows. Are there more of him out there? Are you in mortal danger?* Oddly, his father's voice in his head sounded fainter than before, and Baltasar wondered if a spell was being cast on him, preventing him from hearing his parent's well-intentioned warnings in his mind.

"You only see the willows through the fog, Papa," Baltasar whispered, choking back more tears from the pain that seemed to well up from a place much, much deeper than the skin and muscle so recently abused by the rod. "I'm in no danger here. Don't worry, I'm coming home, and I swear I'll never leave you again."

Just as the silhouette of his beloved cottage broke through the darkness, a fading image assailed his mind. The Erl-king's final offer, lovingly made.

The image Baltasar saw was of himself: enhanced, blooming, sitting on the feathered horse and awash in color, with the Erl-king riding behind him and holding him close. In this vision, he saw that his body had filled out, once-protruding bones sinking under developed muscles, formerly bloodless flesh taking on a rosy hue. In this vision, he sensed himself no longer despairing over his flawed form. He could feel the wind more keenly, the touch of his lover's hands against his waist and the press of the Erl-king's lips against his neck more vividly as he allowed himself to be taken away. In this vision, the feathered horse took a sharp turn away from the path he was now taking, and all three vanished from the world forever.

Demon! Baltasar shook off the tempting image with a fierce prayer.

"I can deny you just as painfully as you've denied me," the Erl-king said before silence widened the chasm between them. Where was he? Baltasar glanced back over his shoulder and found him riding not too far behind, his eyes wide and alight with fading hope and so much pain. Baltasar shook his head, but for what reason, he didn't know. Was he slowing down as well?

Baltasar trembled, his gaze still fixed on the Erl-king, though his own horse thundered toward his home, toward safety.

*He's hurting you! Tell him to go away! You don't need him in your life! Do as I say, you weak, sniveling idiot, or...*

Too late, too late, Baltasar's mind screamed, and he drove his poor horse on, the animal almost stumbling to its death from the extremity of its efforts. He didn't know when he decided to let go of the reins, but he did somehow, and before long he felt himself flying in the night, caught up in the sudden gust of cold wind that blew around him. The world spun, light and color melted into each other, the sharp, invigorating smell of the fresh night air filled his lungs even as he screamed.

"I'll never hurt you," the voice said, and Baltasar pinched his eyes shut as he readied himself for Death, whom he expected to claim him in a few seconds.

Weightlessness gradually faded, and the dizzying motion of a spinning world stopped, to be replaced by a rhythmic gallop that slowed to a gentle canter. The chill air was replaced by warmth and closeness, the terrifying howl of the wind now the gentle hushing of a voice in his ear.

Baltasar waited till the feeling of faintness left him, then he opened his eyes to find himself sitting astride another horse, facing backward, clinging to his lover, who held him fast against himself and who soothed him with quiet words in a tongue he didn't recognize. It must be the language of the wood, he thought, and he stayed there for some time, waiting for his breath and his heart to steady themselves. It was a strange but luxurious and comforting feeling, being embraced by an immortal, a spirit of Nature.

The horse they rode turned, changing its direction back toward the dark wood. Baltasar peered over the Erl-king's shoulder and watched as his riderless horse galloped toward his parents' cottage. It slowed its gait as it neared, not once deviating from its tracks, and Baltasar suspected something had used its influence on the animal, urging it to slow down and stop several feet from the front door and stay there, snorting and neighing, perhaps.

The front door opened, and Baltasar decided not to watch anymore. He'd made his choice, and he was ready for what awaited him afterward. He closed his eyes and reveled in the scents of trees, flowers, and water in the Erl-king's robes.

"Teach me your language," he said tiredly.

"I will."

*What have you done to my son? Where is he, you damned monster?*

"Gone," the Erl-king seemed to say from an indeterminable distance, "gone forever with me."

Age permeated the morning air and thickened it. The heavier scents of old fabric, old paint, and old wood, overcame those of popcorn and cotton candy. The old smells reminded Simon of his grandparents' house. Grass and earth aromas filled his nostrils as well, and the boy thought of the tiny and badly-kept garden of which his grandmother used to be so proud. Were it not for the montage of laughter, conversation, music, and clanking rides within the carnival grounds, Simon would have believed himself back in that bare and humble little home and in his late grandparents' company.

He stared at the barker in the bright red and yellow-striped suit. The boisterous man accosted carnival goers as they walked up to him, tickets in hand. He exchanged pleasantries with the adults, who laughed in their turn. He startled the children, however, and even frightened some of them. The barker didn't seem to notice and greeted them with a hearty shake of a hand for the boys and a little plastic daisy for the girls.

Simon tightened his hold on his mother's hand. "Ma?"

He looked up into familiar eyes of green—young and yet tired. A halo of mouse-brown curls framed her face, which she'd secured with a scarf that made her look older, especially with the large knot under her chin. Simon's sister often joked that their mother must have been a Russian peasant in a past life.

"Are you ready, honey?" She crouched down with a wide smile. From her frayed tote bag, she pulled out the homemade stuffed bear. Money had always been hard to come by, and Simon was raised in everything plain, basic, and second-hand. Caesar was sewn by his mother the year his father was laid off, and Simon had asked for a train set for his birthday. "Hold on to Caesar now."

Simon held the doll tightly. The familiar feel of the toy pressing against his bony chest and its musty scent offered him comfort in the midst of a strange and frightening environment.

"Okay," he said and received a kiss on the cheek.

Simon's father stood a few feet away, waiting and watching, his expression unreadable. He was an imposing figure—broad-shouldered and bronzed from all those hours spent working on roadways, towering well above his wife and keeping the peace with a mere look. Dark-eyed and thin-lipped, he found a softer and quieter doppelgänger in his daughter, who inherited her mother's hair and temperament and her father's dark features. Amy waited beside him with her hand securely in his as she watched her younger brother.

Simon's mother stood up, spoke a few words to her husband, and led the five-year-old boy to the carnival entrance.

"Welcome, ladies and gentlemen, boys and girls!" The barker yelled at the crowd over her head as he took her ticket and tore it in two, giving her half back. "Come right in and find magic! Ride the Venetian Carousel or fly on the Yo-Yo! Try your luck at our shooting galleries and find your way through the maze of mirrors! We have special treats waiting for you today!"

The man's garish attire held Simon spellbound. The boy stood on tiptoes when he presented his ticket, his eyes aglow with expectation as he watched it get torn in two.

"Here you go, young man, and mind yourself." The barker grinned as he handed half back to the boy. He held out a large, ungainly hand. Simon took it and shyly marveled at the huge, sunburnt fingers as they shook hands.

The barker paused and glanced up at the sky. The vast expanse above them was a brilliant cover of blue that seemed to fade into white as it stretched farther and farther into the horizon. Scattered white clouds broke the azure ceiling.

"Looks like rain," the barker muttered.

"I don't see rain clouds."

"They'll be coming soon enough." The barker looked down and smiled once more at the child. "Will rain spoil your day, young man?"

"No. Ma says the sun's just hiding behind the clouds when it rains."

"Your ma knows best. Keep that in mind." He winked and then turned his attention to the next person in line.

Simon followed his family past the entrance and into the confusing yet cheerful hubbub of the carnival grounds. He stared in awe at the throng of laughing people, their hands full with large swirls of rainbow-colored cotton candy or gigantic toys won at the different game booths. Faces flushed, eyes sparkled, mouths set in wide grins, the sounds of light conversation and laughter filling the air, interspersed with the ringing of bells, the clanking of machinery, and the POP! POP! POP! of the shooting gallery. Faint music served as a whimsical backdrop to the confusion. Within minutes, Simon was taking his sister's lead and was begging his parents to take him here and there as he worked hard to sample every single offering the carnival had. The treats, the rides, the games—they all seemed to go on forever, and more than once, Simon was scolded for holding the family up with his pleas to play this or ride that. He didn't care about time, anyway, which he barely noticed was marked by his mother's request for a brief rest every now and then. His family could have been there for days, for all he knew, and it wouldn't have mattered to him.

He even barely paid attention to the smell of rain that was growing sharper and sharper as they wandered farther into the carnival grounds. His mother mentioned it twice, maybe more, but her voice remained faint and distant, nothing more than gentle music that was overwhelmed by the louder and more immediate noise of the carnival.

Deeper into the grounds stood the Venetian carousel, clearly one of the carnival's highlights. It towered with two levels of plumed dancing horses and intricate ornamentation covering the central column, ceiling, and pillars. Colors in every shade of the rainbow were tempered by the softer, more antiquated touches of gold, lending the ride a distinct archaic air. A faint waltz could be heard as the carousel spun, beckoning the children with its sweet strains.

A sudden gust of wind sliced through the crowd. Simon and his mother looked up, noting the thick, dark clouds above them. "Looks like the rain's here. I think you should stay on the carousel to keep yourself from getting wet," his mother said. "I'll have to tell your father and sister to follow us."

Keeping pace with his mother, Simon pushed his way through the crowd until they caught up with his father and sister.

"The children should stay on the ride," his mother called above the din, and her husband nodded.

"What about you?" Simon asked as he and his sister were ushered toward the gate. "Where will you be?"

"We'll be out here. You've got Amy to keep you company, anyway, but stay on the bottom level, all right?"

"But won't you get wet?"

His mother squeezed his hand gently and regarded him with a little smile. "Your father and I can take care of ourselves, honey." Simon was surrendered to his sister, and the deluge began.

The rain came in gradual drops, sprinkling over the carnival for the first five seconds before giving way to a near torrent. Everywhere cries of surprise and dismay rose as people scrambled for shelter.

"Go! Simon! Get on the carousel!"

"Ma!"

"Now!"

Feeling his sister's grip tighten around his hand, Simon elbowed his way through the mass of squealing children as they, too, ran toward the waiting comfort of the carousel while crying for their parents. Simon stole a glance over his shoulder and could see nothing but confusion behind the gates as people ran back and forth. The carnival workers assigned to the carousel seemed to be the only ones untouched, and they carried on with their task in spite of the rain, instructing parents and children where to go and what to do.

Simon and his sister reached the ride and clambered onto the first level, panting and just lightly wet.

"Stay here," Amy said as she took her brother under his arms and hoisted him on top of a prancing horse in green and gold. "Grab hold of the bars and don't *ever* let go, okay?"

"Where are you going?"

"There aren't enough horses here for me," Amy said. "I have to get off. They won't let anyone stand around here and just watch. It's not safe."

"But—"

"Simon, you'll be okay. I'll be waiting for you outside the gate. You won't miss me."

Simon nodded and held Caesar close. "Okay. Just don't leave."

"I won't. I'll never leave you," Amy whispered. Then she gave his hand a quick squeeze and hurried off just when the bell rang to signal to start of the ride.

Simon watched Amy disappear in the rain just when the carousel creaked into motion. Flamboyant horses frozen in mid-canter began to rise and dip in time with the waltz. Shapes and colors swirled as the carousel picked up speed, and Simon clung to his ride, taking comfort in Caesar's homemade presence and everything he'd always associated with the stuffed toy. Beyond the edge of the platform hovered the dour grayness of the rain, the drops blending with the colors of the carnival to form a rough tapestry of shapes and movement.

The ride soothed the boy. Initial misgivings soon gave way to childish wonder at the lights and angels that decorated the central column. A series of narrow mirror panels caught and reflected color and light from all around, providing a stark brilliance to the ride that made Simon blink.

Awash in sound, color, and movement, Simon floated in space, connected with all senses to the carousel and protected from the cold and grayness that filled the world beyond the rotating platform. The illusions eventually dissipated at the conclusion of the ride, however, and the boy was obliged to return to the present when his horse slowed, gently dipping and rising one final time before coming to a full stop in mid-dance, its head bowed.

The waltz faded into the distance. Children began to talk at once, replacing the music with excited chattering as they all shimmied down from their horses to hurry off the platform and run into their parents' waiting arms.

Simon followed. He took in the sight of the wet fairgrounds and the drenched crowd, pleased that the rains had stopped. He was pushed and shoved as he walked toward the gate, craning his neck to catch sight of his sister or parents. Amid the bustling figures of sodden visitors, though, he saw no one he recognized, and it seemed as though many of the children were going through the same thing.

Plaintive calls for parents were soon heard amid the sounds of the carnival, and Simon saw several children break down and cry as they stumbled through the crowd, pale and terrified as they searched.

"Ma?" he called out. "Pa? Amy?" He turned around, circled the carousel, but to no avail.

Everywhere, he found nothing but an endless sea of people, pale and wan in some cases, haggard and weary in others. Hair and clothing both ruined by the rain, the deluge diminishing the light that once shone in their eyes and the irrepressible smiles that once lit their faces. Creases and lines appeared, marking the downturn of mouths and the shadowing of eyes. Those holding cotton candy had their hands covered in colorful melted sugar that clung to their fingers and palms in sticky gobs. Toys won in different game booths were carried around in drooping piles, colorful ribbons dangling off them in lifeless streamers.

Simon glanced up and found the rain clouds still there. They were sagging under the weight of so much collected moisture and could burst any minute now. A fleeting break in the gray expanse, however, offered him a glimpse of the sky beyond, peeking through the little hole in the clouds in a reassuring swatch of blue.

Simon decided to plant himself in one spot in hopes of having his family stumble across him as they searched. They *should* be looking for him. They were likely forced to find shelter in one of the nearby tents and were wandering the carnival grounds now.

Simon, now ten years old, took his place just off the main walkway and away from nearby booths, watching the crowd as they jostled their way about. His damp clothes were beginning to feel cold against his slight body, and he held Caesar close in spite of his embarrassment at still having the toy with him at his age.

There he waited and watched, his heart growing heavier with every passing minute. Men and women walked before him in a confused mass, some searching for friends and family, others dragging reluctant companions along. There were those who seemed to have retained their humor, however, and those were the ones Simon watched all the more closely, taking some measure of comfort in their laughter and conversation. But there were too many of the others—the sadder ones. There were too many. Every so often a child would appear, wailing for his or her parents.

Simon grew restless, the ever-present threat of rain compounding his anxiety. Then he saw a flash of pink and yellow flowers on a skirt.

"Ma!" he cried, darting forward and tripping on other people's feet. He picked himself up from the mud each time, his eyes fixed on the disappearing swatch of cotton. "Ma!"

He finally caught up and, reaching out, gave the skirt a forceful tug as he looked up. The figure whirled around. "What the...?" the woman exclaimed. "Oh, you're filthy!"

Simon flinched. "I thought you were my mother."

"Well, I'm not. You should go to that man over there. He can probably help you." The woman pointed at a clown who stood nearby, entertaining a small group of people with some magic tricks beside one of the tents.

Simon hesitated. He didn't know to what extent clowns were allowed to help lost children. He would have voiced his opinion had the woman remained behind. When he turned to speak with her, she'd already gone, and he was standing in the middle of the crowd, jostled and cursed for being in people's way.

"You're lost, too?" a small voice asked.

Simon looked around and found himself face-to-face with another boy around his age, possibly younger and no less mud-spattered.

"I am."

"Do you want to look for our parents together?"

Simon frowned. He was caught off-guard not so much by the question but by the way the other boy's eyes seemed to flicker in the growing gloom. They were of a rich blue that pierced the drabness of everything else around them. Simon instinctively glanced up, goaded on by a subtle twang in his gut, and saw that the clouds had thickened, the gray canopy on the verge of bursting once again. And, much to his surprise, he saw yet another small break in the clouds, the blue sky filtering through.

"I guess so," he replied. "I think it's going to rain again. Are you looking for your mother and father and sister, too?"

The other boy shook his head ruefully. "Only my father. I don't have a mother. She died a long time ago. I have sisters, though."

"Oh. Okay. Come on then. What's your name?"

"Brian. What about you?"

"Simon."

Simon shifted Caesar as far away from his new companion as possible. He was too old for toys now. Hopefully Brian wouldn't be asking too many questions about Caesar. They moved through the crowd, which was now growing more agitated as the skies dimmed further. Anticipating another downpour, people began to scramble for shelter, a number of them cursing loudly at their luck.

The children stumbled on and managed to make their way past half a dozen tents when the next sheet of rain struck the fairgrounds. Soon the two were huddled together behind the flaps of the little tent that housed the mechanical fortune-teller. They were small enough to fit, which made it convenient for them as they'd seen the crammed interiors of the larger tents, with people packed in a soaked cluster as they waited miserably for the rain to subside.

"Oh, look," Brian said as he picked up a muddy piece of paper lying by his sneakers.

"Don't touch it," Simon retorted. "It's dirty."

"No, look—it's a fortune."

They stared at the little strip of cheap paper and its barely discernible print.

*You're contemplative these days, pondering the spring skies, deconstructing songs, and finding magical worlds in the eyes of those around you. If you tend this particular garden, it'll grow. Don't let anyone tell you it's not worth the trouble.*

"I don't get it." Simon sighed. "Those things are stupid, anyway."

Brian snickered and picked up another piece of paper.

"Stop that."

Brian grinned. "I'll bet you this one's about you." When Simon rolled his eyes and snorted, he laughed and held it up, reading it aloud and stumbling over some of the words.

*You've tried puffing out your chest, donning disguises and even acquiring a new vocabulary, yet nothing you do seems to get the results you want. If all else fails, be yourself. You'll get under the skin of those who're demanding that you change, and your self-possession will be an inspiration to someone who holds you in high regard.*

The two teenagers fell silent as they stared at each other.

"I told you those are stupid."

"I guess you're right. My sisters read them all the time, though."

Simon shrugged. "We're too old for this shit."

"Oh, like that teddy bear?"

"Shut up. I'd lose this thing if I could."

"Dude, you're *sixteen*. What're you doing with a stuffed doll?"

"Look, I'll get rid of this thing once I get the chance. If you see a little girl, let me know. She can have this with my blessing. Now shut the fuck up."

A young face, now in the process of shedding its softness for an adult's firm features, broke out in laughter, blue eyes still bright against the bleakness. Simon couldn't help but marvel at its shifting beauty as he stared back in silence.

"Here. I think you should keep these." The muddy fortunes were carefully folded and slipped inside Simon's shirt pocket.

"What for? I don't need them."

"I don't know. Maybe if you hold on to them long enough, you'll believe them."

"But they're not real."

"Color me optimistic, jerk."

"I think you listen to your sisters too much." Simon frowned, but he didn't remove the slips of paper from his pocket.

Brian shrugged, beaming. "I guess it's not too bad being lost, eh?" When Simon didn't answer, he shifted to his hands and knees and crawled cautiously forward to peer through the flaps of the tent. "The rain's still going. How long do you think it'll last?"

"I don't know. Hopefully soon. It's too cramped in here, and we can barely fit." Simon crawled forward as well and took his place beside Brian. Before them he saw several people braving the rain, running or walking at a hurried pace. Their clothes and shoes and prizes were ruined, but they didn't seem to care. Gritting their teeth, they nevertheless carried on with what they wanted to do, urging each other forward when friends and family began to complain about the rain.

"Maybe our families are looking for us right now while the crowd's small," Simon offered.

"Should we go?"

"I can go. You can wait for me here. What does your dad look like?"

Brian shook his head. "No. I'll come with you. It'll be too hard for you to take care of both of us on your own."

"I don't need any help." All other words faltered and died in his throat, his thoughts scrambled and thrown to the four winds, for all of a sudden, Brian was kissing Simon with the clumsy assurance of a confident teenager. It was brief, chaste, and wet, but nothing would ever be the same again the second their mouths pulled away from each other. Simon stared at his companion, completely at a loss.

"Yeah, you do," Brian said without missing a beat. "I'm coming, anyway, and I don't care what you say."

He scrambled to his feet before Simon could say another word, and before long, the two boys were hurrying through the carnival grounds hand in hand. They were shivering and miserable, tired and hungry, dirty and heartsick. But they pushed on, passing by the shooting gallery along the way and staring in amazement at the long line of people who stood in a determined, patient group as they waited their turn. The familiar sounds of POP! POP! POP! mingled with the rhythmic patter of the rain.

The people's faces were grim and even more haggard than before, the light of joy now extinguished from their eyes. The creases on their faces had deepened, the scowls darkened. But they braved the rain and seemed determined to get their money's worth. And when people huddling within the tents nearby saw what they were doing, some of them ventured out to join the others in line, squaring their shoulders against the deluge and allowing themselves to be hammered mercilessly by the stinging cold. Men, women, and even children slowly congregated around the shooting gallery, and before long, the area was once again alive with the sound of lively chatter from those few brave (and some would say foolish) souls.

As Simon scanned the crowd, he caught a glimpse of yellow and purple plaid.

"Dad!" he cried, breaking away from Brian and pushing his way through the crowd.

He found the man and was about to give the wet flannel shirt a tug when the latter turned around to speak with those who were with him. Simon's spirits fell when he found himself once again staring at a stranger, once again orphaned and alone. Where was his family? Had they abandoned him for good? What was he supposed to do now?

He turned around, stunned and shaken. He needed to find Brian. At least he had him, Simon reminded himself. The two of them could stay lost together and find solace in each other's company for as long as they could. Once he reached the spot where he believed he left Brian, he found that his friend was gone.

"Brian?" he called out. "Hey, Brian!"

The rain had abated. He sneezed and shivered as he hurried on, calling out his friend's name this time. He wove his way through the smaller walkways, navigating around booths and tents. Nothing answered his calls but carnival music and the cacophony of unfamiliar voices.

Exhaustion finally overcame him, and he sat on a wet bench somewhere in the midst of mud, rain, and drooping tents. He looked around, numbed, before he became aware of the soiled and faded toy in his hand. He held up Caesar and stared long and hard at the homemade bear. A surge of anger tempted him to rip the thing apart, to enjoy the feeling of fabric and thread tearing under his fingers, the sound of his childhood being shredded, the sight of old cloth remnants flying all over as his past was gradually and inexorably gutted till nothing was left.

He pressed his fingers against the doll's soft belly. Then Simon hesitated. It was Caesar, after all, he was about to destroy. Caesar was his childhood companion and his best friend when he was punished. Though consigned to the dustiest corner of his room once Simon had outgrown toys, it was his confidant, the asymmetrical ears a ready receptacle of his pre-pubescent secrets. It was his retreat, the soiled and floppy body willingly shouldering Simon's guilt-ridden and lonely fantasies from where it sat in the corner as the teenager stroked himself to completion with the images of other boys and men smiling seductively at him in his mind. It was his personal hell, the hand-sewn seams holding up to his punches and the occasional flight across the bedroom as he threw it around after he came out to his family when he was seventeen, and his world collapsed because he was dead in his father's eyes.

Simon wasn't even aware of his tears till he heard the voice, and he looked up to find his vision blurred by moisture.

"Rain sucks fat donkey balls, doesn't it?"

A clown stood before him. His makeup had run from the rain, with red, green, and blue streaks marring his white mask in colorful tears. Simon stared at him cautiously as the clown smiled in spite of his ruined face. The boy recognized him as the one who was entertaining the newly drenched crowd after the first deluge.

"I can take you to security. That okay with you, or am I asking the obvious?"

Simon nodded and chuckled. "I didn't even think about security," he replied tiredly. "It just feels like forever since I lost my way."

"Hey, that's all right. Sometimes it takes a while to figure things out—especially in situations like this. How old are you, anyway, kid?"

"Twenty going on fifty."

"Twenty, huh? Interesting friend you've got in your hands."

"That's Caesar." Simon shrugged.

The clown laughed and patted Simon's shoulder as the young man stood up, relieved and hopeful. "Come on. I'm guessing that you don't need security's help at this point, but the exit's not too far." He paused and frowned, narrowing his eyes as he stared long and hard at Simon. "What the hell happened to you?"

Simon gingerly touched his left cheek and winced at the mild pain that throbbed in the tender area. His mouth was swollen, his lower lip cut. "I got beaten up." Gay-bashed would have been more specific, but Simon didn't care to elaborate.

"Beaten up? What for?" the clown prodded. Then realization seemed to dawn, and he blinked then nodded. "Come on, kid. The exit's this way."

The rain had finally stopped. A quick glance at the sky showed several breaks in the clouds now, with the sun's rays filtering through every yawning gap in the heavy grayness above. Patches of bright blue peeked out as well, familiar signs of reassurance.

The clown led him through the crowd. Simon kept his gaze fixed on the hobbling figure before him and found unexpected comfort in the ruined figure of a man whose job was to entertain and to embody the spirit of the carnival. He thought of Brian. He wondered where his friend was now, wondered how Brian fared after their sudden separation. Simon could still see him, smiling in that foolish, confident way of his. He could still hear Brian's voice. He could still feel Brian's warmth and remember his taste. In spite of everything, Simon regretted nothing. He couldn't imagine what else he would have done with his life if not embrace it, carnival and rain and all.

Around him the carnival came alive. The survivors of the rain resumed their exploration of the area. Music continued to fill the air, and conversation and laughter broke through the dampness. Life, as it were, simply went on.

Simon and his guide reached the carnival's exit. They stopped, and the clown turned and pointed at the gate. Simon regarded the rain-marred face for the last time, taking note of the way the ruined colors dried up in what seemed to be permanent scars on the white, waxy mask, colorful tears that cut through the surface and served as lifelong reminders of light, music, laughter, and rain.

"Listen," the clown said, "you'll be okay. If you walk out that gate, you'll find people waiting out there to help you."

"Thank you. I really appreciate it."

"No problem, buddy. Good luck."

Simon followed the scattered groups of people who were also making their way to the exit. He passed through the gate and stood outside the carnival grounds, looking around him. The sky was still overcast. The patches of blue still beckoned to him. But the world seemed different—changed. He couldn't quite place a finger on it as he gazed around, watching people walk off, with some being reunited with friends and family and lovers at long last.

He stood in some confusion for several seconds before he heard his name called, and he turned to find a woman standing nearby, smiling at him. She must be in her late thirties, reddish-brown hair set in loose curls that framed her face, her eyes echoing a familiar pair from his past. Yes, they were his father's eyes, he thought. But her smile was very much like his mother's.

Simon, now thirty years old, took a tentative step toward her.

"I told you I'll be waiting outside the gates," Amy said.

Simon hesitated. "Mom and Dad…"

Amy only shook her head and shrugged, regret now tingeing her smile with a distinct sadness. "Mom said she still loved you in spite of how things worked out. She's buried near Grandma and Grandpa. Dad—well—won't talk about you still. I'm sorry."

Simon nodded, pulling his sister close and holding her tightly. "Thanks, Amy."

"Okay," she said as she pulled away and gave him a kiss on the cheek. "Your family's waiting for you. I'm not about to spoil their day. Go on. Shoo."

She gave him a little shove in another direction, and Simon was facing two figures that stood at a distance, clad in raincoats and waving at him.

Those eyes were just as radiant as he remembered—tempered, perhaps, by the pain of loss, but they were incredibly brilliant still, almost teasing in the way they hid behind a pair of designer glasses. The voice was just as cheerful and melodious as it was several years ago.

"Yoko wants pizza for dinner tonight," Brian declared, indicating with a gentle tug of a hand the little girl who stood beside him. "I said yes. I hope it's okay with you."

Simon grinned. "You know I can't refuse you guys anything." He crouched as their adopted daughter pulled away from her other father's grasp and hurried over to him. "What kind of pizza did you have in mind, kiddo?"

"Mushroom? Pineapple?" Yoko paused and then pointed at Simon's hand. "What's that, Daddy?"

"Oh." Simon held up the old, faded stuffed bear. "This is Caesar. Your grandma made him."

"He looks kinda dirty and gross."

"I know he's not much to look at, but he's a good friend. And I think Grandma would've liked you to have him."

Yoko looked dubious at first but eventually gave in, and she took the doll from her father and held it close. "I guess he can get cleaned up for tea."

"He can, of course, and we'll figure something out. Keep him safe now." Simon kissed his daughter, stood up, and led her back to his husband. Brian was busily scanning the sky.

"What's wrong?"

"Looks like rain," Brian replied, and sure enough, the first drops came down. He glanced back at Simon, bemused. "Caught in the downpour again. How typical."

"Funny how life works." Simon chuckled, leaned close, and kissed his husband, not at all feeling the rain.

# The Bridge

Remy Pépin blew out a shuddering breath as he stood inside his little cottage, rubbing his hands up and down his arms and looking around in half-starving misery at the bare and unlit space that made up his home. Cottage, indeed—it was nothing more than a reasonably-sized rectangular space with four walls and a roof. What furniture Remy owned was scattered in as wide an area as possible in a vain effort at eating up enough space and to give the impression that he wasn't terribly poor.

It was vain, yes, for his furniture amounted to nothing more than a weather-beaten bed, a couple of chairs, a rickety table, and an old sideboard luckily big enough to contain his meager clothing and even more meager food supplies, cooking pots, and dishes. Another lucky detail was a large fireplace he maintained with overzealous energy.

Remy snorted as he hurried over to it, dropping to his knees and fumbling around for more wood and the matches. He didn't have much of a choice in this, for that fireplace was his lifeline. He'd be starving to death if he didn't cook, and he'd be freezing to death if he didn't maintain it.

Several frigid, miserable moments passed before happy warmth filled the cottage's interior, and Remy was once again able to relax, sitting before the fireplace with his arms stretched out. Several moments later, the ice that kept his joints from properly functioning had melted, and he was busily stirring some soup in a small pot.

He left the pot in the fire to let it simmer for a few more minutes and began the task of preparing the table for another solitary meal.

As he stood before the sideboard, he caught sight of the candle off to the side, and he paused as he deliberated. Should he light it like he'd done for several nights in a row? Remy winced.

"Mme. Jolicoeur's superstitions are nothing more than that," he chided himself as he set his bowl and spoon aside in favor of the matches. "They mean absolutely nothing." He struck a match and lit the candle, holding one hand close to cup the flame. "They're silly little tales that are meant for nothing more than entertainment."

Taking up the candleholder and still cupping the flame, he carefully walked to the window next to the door. "I'm sure there are a hundred different variations of the same superstition all over the world, and they all mean the same thing—nothing," he continued as he set the candle down on the window ledge. There were no curtains anywhere, for he could barely afford the clothes on his back, and those weren't much to begin with. Wasting precious money on luxuries like curtains was madness.

Remy stood back and watched the candle's little flame flicker cheerfully against the window, the reflection in the glass stirring a familiar pang of hope in his chest. The outside world was dark, with snow falling in an endless curtain.

"No," he said, shaking his head as he turned around and walked back to the sideboard to continue his preparations. "A candle sitting on a window ledge doesn't attract luck. It doesn't bring good spirits to anyone's door. And I sure don't believe it'll work because I'm a great deal too practical."

Remy continued to talk to himself in this vein throughout his meal preparation. Even as he sat down to eat, he kept muttering on and on about superstitions involving candles as beacons of hope in the dark, frigid night and how much he didn't believe them. Such ideas were far too fanciful.

In fact, he was such a skeptic that he'd pause in his meal every so often to glance at the candle or the door, holding his breath and waiting, his heart pounding. His disbelief was so intense that, when a knock shattered the lonely silence of his cottage, Remy leapt up and ran to the door without a moment's thought, swinging the door wide open and staring in numbed shock at the shivering figure standing outside.

"I'm so sorry for bothering you," the young man stammered, deeply flushed and squinting against the wind. "I seemed to have lost my way, and—"

"Please come in," Remy said, stepping aside and waving the stranger in, feeling himself shrink in mortification, for he recognized the boy who entered. "I've just started dinner, but you're more than welcome to join me." He closed the door and struggled a little with the lock, which was a common thing since it was as old as time itself.

The stranger stood in the middle of the cottage, gazing around him, still shivering, and with a pleading look, he wordlessly asked permission to stand before the fire. Remy nodded, and the snow-covered boy hurried over to it, falling to his knees, and sighing as he rubbed his arms before stretching his hands out to warm them.

"I'll get you something to eat," Remy said, still wide-eyed and shocked. "I'm afraid it's not much—just soup with hardly anything in it, but it fills my stomach, and it's quite hot."

His visitor glanced back over his snow-dusted shoulder and offered a rueful smile. "Thank you, I'd appreciate it very much," he said. "You're very kind."

Words failing him, Remy hurried over to the sideboard and pulled out another bowl and spoon and filled it with soup. He stole surreptitious glances at the kneeling figure whose back was turned to him, his embarrassment at being seen in such a miserable light compounding the discomfort of his twisting belly. How could this happen? This unexpected visitor of his—Remy had been hopelessly infatuated with him for so long. What were the chances of him stumbling across Remy's cottage on a miserable winter evening? The possibilities were so absurd, and if Remy weren't so much in shock, he'd have laughed at the situation.

He didn't know his visitor's name, but he was about to find out. He did know the family to whom the young man belonged, though, for Remy had seen him in the company of an older man—perhaps his father or uncle—in the tailor's shop where he worked. From the dusky corner that was his assigned workspace Remy would watch the boy move about, trailing his companion and looking dreadfully bored. Remy didn't know whether his visitor recognized him, but it didn't matter much. The rich never bothered with the poor, anyway, and as the host, it was Remy's duty to ensure his accidental guest was made comfortable, warm, and adequately fed.

Remy hesitated for a few more seconds as he took in the sight, admiring in silence at not only the clear signs of wealth and privilege in his visitor's general appearance, but also the remarkable serendipity of the moment.

"What are the chances?" he kept whispering to himself, shaking his head and wishing he had a friend with him who could pinch him awake. Gathering his courage, he walked over to the other boy and offered the bowl and spoon. "I'm very sorry it's not much," he said, unable to meet the bright, blue-eyed stare and dropping his gaze to the bowl while shrugging. "I'm not used to having guests here."

"It's all right, really. I'd rather have what you're eating than…" The boy paused, and Remy looked up at him in time to catch a faint shadow darkening his features. But it was gone in a breath, and their gazes met, pinning Remy in place. "My uncle's table is always littered with the most expensive food, but his dining room's filled with loud, pointless, empty chatter." He smiled, his eyes twinkling. "I've never been one for tedious company."

"Well, I could very well turn out to be that," Remy said, straightening up, again dropping his gaze in embarrassment. "I'm not exactly known for my polish."

"I sincerely doubt it." The boy set his bowl down and reached out a hand. "I'm Alain Étoile," he said, and Remy shook his hand, hoping Alain wouldn't notice the clamminess or the faint tremor in his hold. "Pleased to meet you…?"

"Remy Pépin. Likewise."

Very carefully, as though handling the most precious gems or glass, Alain took up his bowl and set it a little off to his side before shifting and sitting down this time, crossing his legs under him and resting his elbows against his thighs as he picked up his bowl again. "Would you mind joining me down here?" he said, chuckling and coloring. "Your fire's too comfortable for me to want to go anywhere else."

"But don't you want a chair to sit on? I've got two. I can move them and the table closer to the fire."

Alain watched him for a moment, looking thoughtful, and then shook his head, a faint smile curving his lips. "No, thank you. I'm quite settled, and it's—I don't care to be reminded of being anywhere else but here." He blinked as though confusing himself with what he'd just said. "I'm sorry, I'm babbling nonsense. Please—would you join me on the floor?"

Remy could only nod and hurry off to claim his supper. Before long, the two were sitting before the fire, chatting and exchanging stories about their lives. Happily, neither could share everything about himself, giving rise to the possibility of many more such talks in the future. Remy, at least, held on to that hope, feeling a confusing mix of fear, anxiety, and jubilation at having something he'd always dearly wished within his reach. Throughout their time together, he took care to remain vigilant, looking for signs of revulsion or hesitation in Alain, but he found none. His guest appeared to be happy to talk, drawing out the time as far as he could, flattering Remy with his undivided and sincere attention.

Remy threw in an occasional log to keep the fire going, though in many ways, he felt as though he were also working desperately to keep Alain with him.

Did Mme. Jolicoeur have any silly superstitions involving fireplaces that perpetually burned? Perhaps it was time for Remy to invent one. He stifled a grin at the thought. By the time Alain was obliged to take his leave, it was nearly midnight, and Remy offered to escort him as far as the nearest inn, where Alain could hire himself a horse for an easier and safer trip back home. The innkeeper wouldn't mind, knowing he'd be obliging a member of the Étoile family. That the young man would take it on himself to go out for an evening walk in the snow baffled Remy, but Alain confessed to have done so in the heat of the moment following a quarrel with his uncle.

"I hope he doesn't pay dearly for it," he muttered as he watched horse and rider vanish in the darkness, raising a hand in farewell. The walk back to his cottage wasn't as bad, for there was something nice and warming about being shocked out of one's miserable daily existence through the machinations of Fortune. Even after Remy had cleaned up, stoked the fireplace with the remaining wood, dressed for bed, and crawled under the covers, the remarkable events of the evening remained fixed on the surface of his mind, unable to filter through the thick layer of disbelief and allow him the luxury of happy acceptance.

It took him a while to fall asleep. The last thing he saw was the candle still burning, the little flame flickering erratically against the chill air that whistled through cracks around the window. Eventually it died, and Remy sank into the world of pleasant dreams.

· · · ·

MATHILDE JOLICOEUR recognized the thin, ill-clad figure as it tramped through the snow, stumbling whenever a foot got stuck in the drift, but picking itself up with the determination the bookseller had long grown to admire. Nodding, she returned to her task of sorting through a pile of old volumes she needed to package and send to M. Rivard before the end of the day, for he was her best and most influential patron, and she couldn't afford to lose his business.

With a rueful sigh, she wished her husband were still alive and standing beside her, advising her on the most efficient way of tackling such a monstrous project.

The same ill-clad figure stepped in within moments, pausing to adjust to the warmth of the shop's interior before the visitor staggered forward.

"Ah, M. Pépin!" Mathilde said, smiling her brightest. "Come and warm yourself! I must apologize for the state of my shop, but as you know, I've no good assistants at the moment, with poor Anton down with a fever."

The young man returned her smile, rubbing his hands briskly as he approached the counter and the stacks of books that littered it. Mathilde took note of his tattered gloves and of his fingers poking out when they ought to be protected from the cold. A quick inventory of the visitor's clothes revealed nothing different from what she'd already seen before. Every item of clothing was worn to virtual shreds, with edges frayed, holes patched over, and colors fading into drab shades. The thick scarf wrapped around the neck was doing as poor a job as the gloves in keeping Remy Pépin warm. In fact, the poor youth's ensemble was simply pitiful, Mathilde thought with a Tsk! Tsk! and a slight shaking of her head.

A light dusting of snow powdered the dark, windswept hair, and Remy's complexion was stained with a rosy flush from the sting of cold air. Mathilde sighed and offered him a handkerchief when he sniffled and rubbed his reddened nose.

"No, thank you," he replied, his spirits surprisingly high despite his miserable state. "I'm sure I'll be fine. It's only a slight cold."

"Impervious to foul weather—I've always admired that in you, young man. And what a wretched season we're having right now."

Remy laughed, and Mathilde stared at him. She rarely heard him laugh before, and when he did, it was a quiet, self-conscious outburst. Not now, however-er.

"Monsieur?"

"I'm feeling a bit impervious to everything today, Mme. Jolicoeur," Remy said, his eyes vibrant. "The weather's foul, my stomach's shrunken, my clothes are falling apart even as I wear them, and I don't care."

She frowned, her gaze critical as she watched him flitter among her books, humming to himself, picking up one volume after another to inspect the cover and then setting it back down. The boy was distracted, she concluded, and hopelessly so. She could feel suppressed energy in the air, and was afraid of saying the wrong thing, lest she unwittingly unlock Pandora's Box and let loose a storm of youthful fire that might prove to be difficult to manage.

Mathilde knew what she needed to do. Abandoning her work, she went to the back room, poured some cider into a glass (if her poor husband could see her now!) and returned to the shop with it. She set it down next to the stack of books through which she was sorting. The drink would find its way inside its intended consumer soon enough. Every once in a while, Mathilde would look up and watch Remy as he lost himself in her books, still bubbling over with unusual energy. She frowned, pursing her lips, and presently gave up. He'd have to tell her everything soon enough, or she'd be forced to wring every bit out of him, so help her.

Remy presently grew tired of examining the books and planted himself directly before Mathilde, and he leaned over the counter and rested on his elbows. He was grinning—a bright, irrepressible grin that shocked Mathilde further. She'd always known him as a withdrawn and half-starved orphan, living day to day with no hope in his heart despite his seventeen years. He'd always appear in her shop either before trudging off to work or on the way home, and she'd offer him a momentary respite from the harshness of his life with friendship, easy conversation, and even food and drink whenever she had any to offer. And yet there he was, practically bouncing all over the place.

Her hand flew to her heart in reflexive answer. If this boy were to catch her off-guard with one more surprise, she didn't know if she'd be able to survive it.

"I used to dismiss all the stories my grandmother used to tell me," he said, his voice dropping as though he were sharing a secret. His gaze, burning and alive, held his audience in place, and Mathilde stood frozen in one spot, compelled to listen because now she thought she understood the mystery. "Legends and myths and superstitions—she used to fill my head with those things to keep me from feeling ill or hungry when I was a child. When I heard you talk about some of those stories she shared, I laughed them away. I know better now, though."

"Young man, you're babbling. Are you sure you aren't ill?"

Remy shook his head. "One of the legends or superstitions you talked about involved a candle by the window..."

"Oh, yes. I remember," she replied. "What happened?"

"It's true."

"My dear boy, it's nothing more than superstitious nonsense. It doesn't work, and it isn't true."

"You know where I live, don't you? You know how impossible it is for people to find their way there at night and in the freezing cold. Yet he came, and…"

"Who?"

"He—him. It was an amazing coincidence…" Remy's words faltered as he caught himself, logic finally stirring and clawing its way out of his muddled thoughts. He looked shocked for a second, then he colored deeply, then his energy diminished. "I suppose you're right. It's nonsense. Just some harmless old wives' tale. Coincidences happen all the time, right? There's no such thing as events being manipulated on purpose by someone or something, is there? Like Fortune, for instance? No, no—that's impossible. Nonsense. Old wives' tales are just harmless stories you tell children."

Mathilde smiled and took one of his hands between hers, squeezing it gently. "Monsieur, I was simply entertaining you with all sorts of stories. You've been looking so hopeless lately—I couldn't bear watching you walk around like a miserable little shadow. I didn't think you'd be taking my babbling seriously."

Remy glanced down at his clothes. "Look at me. I can barely keep myself warm with my own clothes. No one wants to spend time with me because I'm too poor to be worth anyone's trouble. All I have are stories and legends." He looked up again, smiling. His energy was now dimmed, but it was still there. "I can't help but believe. Sometimes I feel that I have to."

"I'm sorry. I shouldn't have made light of your situation. If legends prove to be real…"

"I'd like to think this one's real."

"…then I believe you, and it's real." Mathilde gave his hand another squeeze before letting go. She indicated the glass of cider. "Drink this. I know you'll need it, seeing as how you're on your way to work."

Remy nursed his drink, chatting through it all and appearing to recover his cheerfulness again, and Mathilde took great delight in his mood. His conversation was so infectious, in fact, she was forced to abandon her work and help herself to some cider, raising her eyes to the heavens and muttering, "Don't even start with your scolding, my dear. You know I never get drunk. And, no, I'm not trying to get this poor boy drunk, either, let alone teach him a new vice."

She rejoined Remy in the shop and encouraged him to talk some more, and before long, both of them had finished their drinks. Mathilde was as good as her word, for she didn't fill up Remy's glass, and while he might be enjoying the warmth only good cider could give him, he still had his head on right and would be able to go through the awful tedium of his work without the risk of slipping. Well...as long as he didn't allow himself to daydream too much of *him*, of course, but as far as that went, Mathilde had no control over it.

Remy nodded, hope lighting his face once more. "I should go. M. Barrette isn't very forgiving of tardiness."

"The man's not forgiving of life," Mathilde corrected firmly. She never liked Remy's employer, and it was with a pensive air that she watched the boy leave her shop for another soul-crushing day of working for the local tailor. It would be another ten hours of cramped working space, pricked fingers, and sore ears from the cantankerous man's periodic tweaking or boxing as punishment for blunders both real and imagined. Today, however, offered the poor boy some hope, and Mathilde watched him trudge back out into the snow, the ill-clad figure bent from the cold and thin from want—yet Mathilde knew this bit of hope would buffer the hardness that awaited him.

"So long as that happens, I'll be quite easy in my mind," she murmured as Remy disappeared around the corner.

Mathilde returned to her work, losing track of time. An hour or two must have passed before the shop bell rang again, and she looked up to see another familiar figure walking up to the counter, saluting her with a frown.

"Ah. Here we go," she murmured, nodding and smiling at the newcomer.

One of the privileged few was this youth. Untouched by the harshness of labor, he looked more like a golden-haired statue picking its way through the dour throngs of the working-class and the poor. He'd been to the shop before, most of the time to browse through the books, though not as inclined to engage Mathilde in conversation as most other patrons were. He always arrived richly dressed, his features fixed in a thoughtful, oftentimes melancholy look. He was, as far as Mathilde understood, quite unhappy with his own situation, especially now that he'd just turned eighteen, and his family was too keen on matching him up with anyone who didn't fall short of their impossible standards.

So the young man, in spite of his declarations of complete disinterest in any lady, was continually shoved into one disastrous friendship after another.

Mathilde's bookshop turned out to be a most welcome escape for him, who always lost himself in the perusal of poetry.

"M. Étoile," she said with a warm smile. "A pleasure to see you this morning! What can I do for you?"

"Give me the right directions to the road that would take me to Digne-les-Bains," Alain Étoile retorted, brushing snow off the rich texture of his coat and the waves that softly framed his face.

"Oh. I gave you those the other day, didn't I?"

"No, you didn't. What you gave me were directions to some godforsaken corner of this town. I told you when I was here last, Madame, that I needed to get away from here. I'm sick of all the primping and posturing of all those self-absorbed dandies my uncle sees fit to be proper company for me." Here Alain paused, letting out a weary sigh as he shook his head. "I thought I told you all about that the other day."

"And so you did! And I gave you something else entirely?" Mathilde hastily replied in as soothing a tone as she could while fishing around the counter drawers for her writing tablet. She finally found it and pulled it out, quickly flipping through until she found a fresh, clean sheet.

"Yes, you did."

"Oh, dear," she squawked, grimacing. "I'm so sorry, Monsieur, for writing down the wrong information for you—don't know where my head was at that time. I'm so sorry. The road to Digne-les-Bains, you say?" She tore off the clean sheet of paper, wrote the correct directions down, and then handed it over to Alain, smiling sheepishly and wiping the ink off her fingers. "I hope things didn't go badly for you when you went, um..?"

"I went last night."

"Last night."

Alain took the directions from her, his irritation dissipating. "No, I was fine, thank you. Forgive me for being so short. Anyway, I thought I was going to get lost and freeze to death in the night, with no lights to guide me anywhere. But I found this run-down cottage that had a candle lit by the window, and I just had to run to it."

"You didn't take your coach or at least a horse, Monsieur?" Maternal disapproval dripped from every word, and Alain colored as he shrugged.

"I had another quarrel with my uncle, and I needed to get away as quickly as I could," he said. "He refused me the damned coach or even a measly horse. Can you imagine that? He thought doing that would discourage me from running off in the night, but I proved him wrong. He's always wrong, anyway, and I'm always too happy to rub his nose into it."

"Very impetuous of you, young man."

He nodded, looking like a chastised schoolboy. "A fault of mine," he admitted, "but sometimes it brings me some luck. I had your directions with me, and I didn't get too far."

"That character flaw of yours brings you good luck like last night, I presume? Were the people in the cottage helpful?"

"Person—just one. And, yes, he was." A slight smile touched the young man's lips when he fell silent and thoughtful.

"I'm glad."

Alain nodded, looking momentarily embarrassed as though he'd just remembered where he was. For the first time since Mathilde knew him, the proud, imperious boy seemed uncertain, lost in a train of bewildered thoughts—almost like Remy several hours ago, she appended, stifling a grin.

"Well, thank you for the directions, Mme. Jolicoeur," he said. "I should go. My uncle's waiting for me outside, and I told him I wouldn't be long." Alain rolled his eyes wearily, and Mathilde chuckled.

"Should I take the wrong directions back, Monsieur, so you wouldn't confuse the two now you've got both?"

Alain paused by the door, his gloved hand resting on the handle. He stared blankly at her for a second. Then understanding sank in, and he flushed a little, shaking his head. "No, that's not necessary," he replied, another little smile lighting his face with the same half-fearful, half-expectant hope Mathilde had seen in Remy earlier that day. "I can throw the other one away, myself. Thank you."

Without another word, the youth stepped out, and Mathilde watched him walk off and climb inside a waiting carriage. She thought of Remy and his hopeless infatuation with Alain, the look of stunned pleasure when he almost confessed to having Alain with him last night. Quite natural for the boy to be in shock, Mathilde noted while she tidied up her counter, given how many times he'd likely watched Alain from a distance, the young man's uncle being a loyal patron of M. Barrette's business, after all.

She smiled, a bit smug, as she turned her attention back to her work. It was a job well done, she realized, her gaze straying to her writing tablet. Sometimes happy accidents simply needed a slight nudge or two, a well-meant deception here and there. Mathilde tried not to think of Alain Étoile's uncle, but her sympathy for the young men reminded her how it felt to love hopelessly. She knew how it felt being an outsider, and it was an effective enough force for her to accept, though perhaps still not fully understand, the subversive nature of Remy's infatuation and Alain's disinterest in women.

"Tibault Étoile—it was a long time ago, and we were both children," she said, shaking off the memories and straightening her shoulders. "A dashing young man, whose looks young Alain was lucky enough to inherit."

It was a brief, terribly passionate, and doomed romance between a gentleman from an aristocratic line and a young girl who was no more than a merchant's daughter. Mathilde missed Tibault, to be sure, and he'd always remain her first love.

When she fixed her mind on the looks of bewildered pleasure on Alain and Remy's faces, she couldn't help but laugh, her voice light and young in spite of her sixty-odd years, the sound filling her dimly-lit shop.

"These romantics," she hiccoughed, shaking her head indulgently. "They always have their heads in the clouds."

The sound of something falling to the floor broke the silence of the shop, and she looked up to find a couple of large books lying on the ground. Perhaps Remy had dislodged them without knowing it. There was, after all, no logical reason for a pair of perfectly shelved books to physically move themselves out of their spots and tumble to the floor. Mathilde chuckled, shaking her head, as she walked around the counter and toward the books. No, indeed, there was no logical explanation for it, which only left her one alternative.

She stooped down, picked up the books, and shelved them, even rolling her eyes at the choice of books. Both were thick volumes on demon lore and witches, not exactly subtle subjects with which to drive across a certain point. Stepping back, she placed both hands on her hips and looked heavenward again.

"Oh, come along, my dear," she said. "Stop your scolding. You know very well I can't help but play the bridge for those two boys. When I finally see you, mind that I'll be wearing your ears down with an eternity of talk about my matchmaking efforts if you don't stop your nagging."

Her deceased husband seemed to have gotten the hint because wherever he might be in the afterlife, he didn't bother her again in her ongoing—and eventually successful—efforts at bringing two young lovers together. A few months later, in fact, Mathilde had the last laugh, judging from the scandalized blustering of M. Étoile regarding Alain's sudden running off with Remy, their destination remaining unknown to the gossiping town save for Mathilde, who was the one who gave them the directions to freedom.

# The Water-Irises

Hugh LaCaille had no room in his life or, indeed, patience, for anything but science. An intellectually gifted young man, he awed his masters and peers alike with his acumen, carving new roads with theory, which he was more than happy to see proven. His studies became his life, and he never mingled with anyone beyond the classroom or laboratory. At first others were affronted by his snubs; however, they soon grew comfortable with the notion that LaCaille was simply one of those reclusive geniuses and left it at that.

His evenings were spent with his eye pressed firmly against a microscope or a spyglass of some magnificent craftsmanship (one only natural philosophers could understand and wield with any skill). Or they'd be flying by with his nose hopelessly lost between the pages of a weathered book, a quill in an ink-stained hand, ready to be defiled with more of his hurried scribblings.

The mysteries of the universe intrigued him, and he'd taken it on himself one night, as he gazed out his window into the darkness beyond, to make it his lifelong purpose to discover ways of coaxing Nature's secrets from her.

And by and large, he'd managed to do just that. Physical science was blown apart at the seams with ruthless, calculating force from an unmatched mind. The elements were conquered and made to bow under his observations and calculations till nothing was left but a trail of desecration in his wake—or at least he believed so.

LaCaille's fierce and single-minded dedication to his work had brought him a certain measure of notoriety; however, it had also compromised his health more than once, the concept of rest somehow vanishing from his vocabulary despite friends' and colleagues' expressions of concern. It was for this reason that LaCaille found himself unemployed more often than he cared to admit, his bouts of ill-health and the resulting temperamental outbursts jeopardizing his work and his relationship with his peers. LaCaille's most recent illness lasted far too long, and by the time he'd fully recovered, his position had already been given to someone of a more robust constitution.

It was for this exact reason that M. Ignace Fournier, one of the most successful businessmen in the country, purposed to hire him as tutor to young Aubin.

"The boy's grown much too slack with his priorities," M. Fournier thundered, knocking his finely crafted walking stick loudly against the floor. An imposing fellow, he towered over LaCaille though the scholar was a tall young man, and he overshadowed the latter with his massive bulk, which LaCaille secretly mocked as a fitting expression of the man's avarice and ruthless approach to all business dealings.

"Priorities, Monsieur?" he repeated coolly as he regarded his blustering guest.

"Why, the priorities one ought to have to succeed in business, of course!"

"I'm not a man of business, Monsieur, and I'm afraid I don't quite follow you here."

In truth, though, LaCaille did understand what the man meant; he was merely indulging in his advantage over the other, and he couldn't resist an opportunity of toying with an adversary who was clearly at his mercy. As an academic, he despised the uncouth practices of the mercantile sort, merchandise and monetary exchanges being an insult to the human mind and its infinitely superior capacities. Money and goods made up a crass tradition, one that gave succor to baser human instincts. Besides, he was still smarting from the loss of his most recent post, and he couldn't help but wallow in bitterness aimed at the world.

M. Fournier snorted and waved his walking stick under the scholar's nose. "What rubbish!" he cried. "For a man known for his mind, you're ridiculously ignorant of too many things!"

LaCaille looked down his nose at his companion and waited in condescending silence.

"Very well then. My son, to put it bluntly, is turning into a confounded poet and has said, in my face, mind you, that he's no use for business, that money means nothing to him and that industry—and I've never been insulted in all my life—that industry isn't much more than a loathsome cesspool of vulgarity and greed." M. Fournier, red-faced, was forced to stop and catch a breath. "The boy—the devil take his books and all noxious poets in the world—has now fixed all his energies on literary pursuits, convinced—damn this!—that he was made for artistry and nothing else."

LaCaille listened with growing amusement. "The boy seems to have a good head on his shoulders," he observed. "At least he knows what he wants—or, indeed, needs. For a lad his age, that's quite a feat."

"Rubbish! Rubbish! A good head on his shoulders? What, to aspire to be a damned sensualist? His so-called needs, Monsieur, are to learn practical things and facts and to be groomed for commerce. He most certainly doesn't need to go cavorting in the wood for hours on end or to waste precious moments writing childish verses about plants or water or fairy magic. What a grotesque idea! Have you heard of anything more idiotic as this?"

The stout walking stick continued to hammer angrily against the floorboards, and LaCaille felt a crippling headache coming on. All the same, he maintained his composure and listened in icy silence. He was forced to concede, however, to the fact that in matters of art, he and this uncouth businessman shared a common belief. He'd always regarded anything musical, literary, or visual to be nonsensical trifles, playthings for the idle and the vulgar.

"And how, Monsieur, can I help in this matter?" he calmly broke in. "If you desire a life of commerce for your son, shouldn't you be hiring someone of a less academic bent for your purpose? What can a natural philosopher do for him?"

"Discipline, M. LaCaille, discipline. Commerce might be his ultimate purpose, but reaching it would require the kind of discipline only scientific academics are gifted with. I need one that's extreme enough to break the idiotic propensity of his toward the fanciful and romantic."

And, to emphasize this final point further, M. Fournier strode up to the scholar, raised his walking-stick, and firmly tapped it against the young man's chest. "Aubin is sixteen, Monsieur. There's not much time left before I hope to see him working by my side, surpassing me, even, in his skills."

But he really didn't need to go that far to grind home his point. He'd long convinced LaCaille of the benefits of this new endeavor, and the young man was never one to turn down a challenge—particularly one that involved the elevation of all things scientific and factual and the subjugation of coarser sensibilities. Besides, he reveled in the idea that in young Aubin he was going to enjoy the euphoric process of shaping an impressionable mind to his mold. And if he were fortunate enough, he'd have the boy exquisitely fine-tuned to his image, not his father's. Now that would be triumph, indeed!

Of course, there was also that far more urgent issue regarding money, and when M. Fournier apprised him of the gentleman's country retreat where La-Caille was to stay, the prospect of peace, solitude, and fresh air further aiding his health—why, it would be madness to turn down the position.

Within minutes, the two men had reached an agreement, and they shook hands and exchanged dry pleasantries before parting ways, with LaCaille feeling relieved at removing himself from the other's company.

• • • •

LACAILLE'S ARRIVAL at M. Fournier's country retreat in La Bresse was received with not much fanfare, much to the scholar's disappointment. All the same, he'd fixed his mind on his new student, and he found it quite easy to shrug off every extraneous trifle, which included Aubin's warm, though not too enthusiastic, reception.

The house, which was really a summer-cottage, was cozy and snug, with only Aubin and a housekeeper and gardener for its residents. It stood sequestered from the rest of the world in a quiet little corner of the countryside, ensconced among thick groves of trees not too far from the Vosges mountain range, faint paths marking its weak connection with the world beyond. The environment was certainly a far cry from the seedy, sooty dreariness of Paris and the bustling mercantile and intellectual life that marked its daily existence.

The cottage's interior spoke of commerce from ceiling to foundation. It was sparsely yet neatly furnished and adorned, with nothing but the most practical elements being allowed to grace every surface. The most treasured books were journals that neatly contained painstaking and thorough accounts of household expenditures and budgetary concerns. Surpluses and deficits were accurately and carefully catalogued, with every volume labeled by month and year before they were tucked away in dusted shelves. Writing accoutrements were everywhere—all gathered into perfectly organized groups, with quills of various sources and sizes sorted out, inkbottles arranged likewise with the additional category of color. Any other bound volume that didn't involve the Fournier financial logs was a book on economics or other similar or related subjects.

The Spartan severity of the entire thing was enough to make LaCaille's head throb, and the scholar was forced to turn to his personal artifacts for comfort, sighing contentedly at the feel of Georges-Louis Leclerc, Comte de Buffon's *Les Époques de la Nature* in his hands, the familiar smell of discolored paper and fading ink tickling his nostrils. He didn't blame Aubin for turning his bedroom inside out with a wild collection of books on poetry and fiction as well as plants gathered from his daily walks, which he was trying to capture in watercolor.

LaCaille observed his surroundings with blasé interest. In his eyes, it wasn't Arcadia that enveloped him in an eager embrace; rather, it was a collection of plant and animal breeds mingled in relative harmony, doing what different species were created to do—subsist on other plants and animals as dictated by Nature, with their equivalent biological-chemical-physical formulas directing their respective courses and nothing more.

Aubin, on the other hand, spared none of his youthful energy in emphasizing the more romantic nature of Nature.

During a morning ramble, they came across a collection of bluebells, one that carpeted the ground in a vivid cluster, enticing the adventurer toward the first line of trees that marked the wood. Aubin eagerly pointed out the bright flowers to his companion and declared with much confidence that they bowed from the weight of the constancy that was their symbol. And when LaCaille firmly corrected him with factual details involving the flowers' physical structure and the resulting curvature of their form, Aubin merely shrugged and laughed before dashing off to fall on his knees in the midst of the flowers, happily taking them in his hands and savoring their texture with fond caresses between his fingers. The tutor, for his part, was left in bewildered silence as he stood on the trail, staring at his young charge as the latter reveled in his senses—touching, smelling, kissing, and murmuring something into the flowers—most likely something poetic and silly, much to LaCaille's embarrassment. He was forced to command the wayward lad back to his side.

Further down the path, Aubin made them pause in their tracks to listen to the birds, ending their auditory experience with a sigh of contentment and a dreamy note regarding birds being troubadours sent down from heaven. For LaCaille's part, birds were nothing more than feathered vertebrates with two of their limbs being fashioned into wings. But Aubin didn't seem to hear him. His attention was wholly fixed on the light songs that continued to fill their air, and Aubin looked up with a beatific smile brightening his features. His complexion took on a soft glow; his eyes were distant and bright; his mouth was lightly parted as though in an expression of awe.

Inside the wood, he led his tutor to different crystalline brooks and streams, noting the graceful manner with which they carved labyrinthine paths through the trees and beyond. Several times, Aubin left his companion's side to lie down by the bubbling water to peer intently into its depths or to press his ear against the grass that lined its edges. They spoke to him, Aubin observed, his eyes dancing. Their voices often beckoned to him, and he went further to explain the reason behind certain reflections cast on the water's surface.

"They're not on the surface," he said emphatically as he stared into a brook. "They come from under the water, and they're really pictures of what goes on inside."

"Inside what?"

"Why, inside the water, of course!"

Aubin smiled in a clear show of confidence in his acumen, while LaCaille frowned. The scholar couldn't wrap his mind around these extravagant and dangerously childish notions the boy insisted on entertaining.

"And what makes you so certain of this, Aubin?" he asked irritably.

"Aelfric said so."

"And who, pray, is Aelfric?"

"A friend," Aubin replied matter-of-factly, with that simple openness that could only be expected from one who didn't keep secrets.

"Ah. I see. And when will this young man honor me with his presence?"

The boy paused, frowning slightly as he thought things over. "Well—I'll have to ask him. He's quite shy of strangers, really, though I've told him not to hide too much from the world. He's very beautiful, and I'm sure you'll agree with me when you lay eyes on him. He doesn't believe me when I say so—only laughs and turns away before I'm done speaking."

"Interesting fellow. Perhaps someday he'll be persuaded to meet me."

"Perhaps. I'll certainly tell him you're keen on being introduced." Then Aubin broke out in a bright, winning smile, effectively killing all stern and disapproving sentiments that were poised on his tutor's lips, and he walked on ahead, losing himself again in his imagination as he experienced the world around him with unabashed sensuality.

From his academic distance, LaCaille watched Aubin interact with his environment—or, rather, make love with his environment. And it was with a mortified flush that the young man realized this though he couldn't tear his eyes off the lad even if he tried. It seemed no surface remained untouched by Aubin. Hands reached out and gently lingered over the moss-eaten and crumbling bark of ancient trees, their fingers tracing every inch with languid fascination.

At times Aubin leaned down and brought his face closer to the object, and he inspected it more critically with lightly furrowed brows and a more insistent surface exploration by his hands. He sometimes inhaled deeply, his eyes fluttering shut as he took in woodland scent, his body responding with a shudder as it filled itself with rich, clear, organic essences. And when he pulled away to move on, a faint smile of pleasure impressed itself on his features, which to LaCaille, seemed to deepen more and more in odd beauty as they ventured further into the wood. To be sure, after walking a bit of a distance, the science master began to entertain strange questions regarding Aubin's existence. The deeper into the trees they wandered, the more Aubin seemed to turn into something supernatural—a woodland spirit, superstitious minds would be apt to note.

There was a change—a shift—vague and fleeting, yes, but there was enough strength in it to affect one's senses on a deeper, more intuitive level. And LaCaille, in spite of his natural turn for fact, science, and mathematics, was hardpressed to deny the strange discomfiture that had begun to stir within him as he kept his hawk-like vigil over the boy.

Aubin's figure subtly, gradually, took on a faint shimmer as it plowed through the gathering mist between the trees. His pale complexion lightened just as the flaxen strands of hair on his head deepened into a richer hue, and he was moving through the shifting gloom like a fairy beacon, glowing softly as though to provide some necessary light and guidance to his perplexed and mesmerized tutor.

"Nonsense!" LaCaille snorted, shaking his head vehemently. "All this ridiculous talk of watery kingdoms and whispering brooks and enchanted birds is putting me in a muddle."

And so, to tear himself away from Aubin's odd, hypnotic lure, he forced his mind on currently unsolvable equations in the realm of physics. He settled down into a comfortable and familiar situation as he deftly wove his way past numbers and formulas and systems, grappling valiantly with abstractions. Before long, he was striding with much greater confidence behind Aubin, the far-away gaze of his more indicative of scientific visions than of romantic ones.

Reality intruded harshly on their eventual return to the cottage, and La-Caille once again reminded himself to impose strict discipline on the boy. The evening then was spent in a long, systematic planning of the following day's lessons.

One curious thing he also managed to observe was the way the cottage and everything in it seemed to crush Aubin's spirits the moment he stepped across the threshold. Like a force that waited for its chance with all the patience of something that lived an eternity, it descended on the lad with stealthy pressure—so much so that Aubin's behavior and mood suffered a gradual though clear change from one of youthful and carefree joy to a more somber and almost aged pensiveness. His loquacity diminished, and he refrained from tossing in extraneous matter in their conversation, keeping his focus on what seemed to be important at that given moment. Aubin turned wan and melancholy though he still smiled for his tutor, but there was certainly a definite air of longing in his manner, made all the more palpable with his occasional glances in the direction of any window and the thoughtful stare that made him lose momentary track of the present dialogue.

"Well, I wasn't hired to encourage his fancy," LaCaille told himself, effectively stilling a quiet voice at the back of his mind—one that had been subtly nagging him with gentle reproaches and reminders of compassion for the friendless and isolated boy. "I'm here to teach him, and I won't leave till I see results—even if I fall sick for all my trouble."

And so the lessons began.

• • • •

YOUNG AUBIN PROVED to be an able student. He had the ability to absorb a good amount of information, but the boy didn't apply himself to his lessons completely. LaCaille's greatest frustration lay in Aubin's willingness to go only so far—enough to satisfy the most basic requirements from his tutor—before he shut himself from any more lessons, losing himself in his own daydreams instead. And when LaCaille demanded more from his pupil, Aubin stumbled and sometimes even resisted with a petulant little protest, and the day's efforts were in danger of being wasted altogether.

LaCaille refused to flog the boy in spite of orders from Ignace Fournier to make liberal use of the cane should Aubin prove to be stubborn or truculent during his lessons. Beatings were barbaric, he'd always said, and the one true path toward enlightenment lay in the stimulation of the mind, not the brutish mishandling of the body.

"Nothing can be gained from a bruised bottom and scarred emotions," he told himself as he watched Aubin half-heartedly work his way through his writing exercises, bright head bent low, pale fingers maneuvering the quill with dogged effort across sheets of paper.

It was with some reluctance as well that LaCaille allowed Aubin to wander off to the wood after his lessons. He felt those solitary rambles only stoked the boy's romantic predilections and therefore exacerbated his daydreams during his hours spent with his tutor. All the same, however, LaCaille couldn't find it in himself to deny him, feeling a curious pang at the sight of Aubin walking alone, a lad who was at an age that required much more than a sequestered lifestyle. Aubin's deprivation gnawed steadily at him, and in spite of his natural tendency to reprove and to enforce his own brand of near-ascetic discipline beyond the classroom, his conscience gave way to pity, and he grudgingly turned to his scientific tracts the moment Aubin hurried out of the cottage and disappeared through the trees.

"I hope he'll at least take advantage of this free time to apply some of the lessons he learned," LaCaille sighed with a shake of his head. "To be sure, the variety of plant breeds out there is enough to encourage him."

It was a hope that remained unfulfilled.

After several days of this, Aubin began to return home with some of the most fantastic stories that could be told, alarming his tutor.

"I've just been to the haven of the water-sprites," he eagerly declared over supper. He seemed too excited to eat, and he spent much of his time toying with his food, picking at it till not much more than shredded meat and vegetables lay in a pile on his plate. Nothing LaCaille said could get him to stop. "Aelfric showed me, at last, after I begged him for so long. The journey into the water wasn't as frightening as I'd expected. I thought I was about to drown, but he took care of me all the way there and back, and he promised to show me more if I wished it."

It was all LaCaille could do to stare at his flushed and unusually cheerful pupil in stunned silence.

"You should have been there with me, Monsieur. When I reached the bottom of the pond, I saw it wasn't just mud and weeds and all other sorts of dull plants that awaited me. There were birds of silver that flew above, and they dropped their feathers wherever they went. The grass was littered with them, and I would have taken some home to show you had Aelfric not kept me from doing so. He showed me the trees in his kingdom, and they were made of bronze- and gold-colored glass. When you touch their leaves, they feel like silk, and they tinkle like a thousand tiny bells. The fruit they bore were made of red glass, and they tasted like the sweet cakes my mother used to make for me before she died."

"What—you ate glass?"

Aubin nodded and carried on, unperturbed. "Aelfric's palace wasn't a real palace—it was a forest of glass trees and velvet flowers, and I met the water-sprites, who were very pretty with all the water-irises in their hair, and they all gave me a kiss on my cheek before they celebrated Aelfric's return with several dances. A nightingale sang for us, and reeds played their music till they were out of breath. It was quite warm there, but the breeze cooled me enough to put me to sleep on the grass. Aelfric woke me up eventually and kissed..."

Aubin abruptly broke off, looked mortified all of a sudden, and, flushing deeply, muttered something about walking back home as he began to shovel the sad remains of his supper in his mouth. LaCaille scowled at his pupil.

This didn't look good at all. Aubin's father was expected back for a visit in a week, and he certainly didn't need to see him indulging in these wild fantasies. The boy would be in deep trouble. LaCaille would be in even greater trouble. The scholar groaned, rubbing his temples, as he considered the prospects. After a month of intensive study, he didn't have much to show his employer; if anything, his presence seemed to have worsened Aubin's poetic tendencies.

"Oh, damn the world," he grumbled before finishing his supper in uneasy silence.

• • • •

LACAILLE REDOUBLED his efforts at instilling discipline in his student. The lessons grew more challenging, and they lasted longer. He made sure to be more exacting in his standards, even placing a cold distance between himself and Aubin both within the classroom and without, his conversation turning clipped and icy and more demanding of the boy. He fought the quiet voice of his conscience again and again as he watched Aubin struggle with his lessons, growing more despondent with his inability to keep up with the grueling pace and flinging himself further into his daydreams whenever the pressure proved to be too great of a burden.

"He has to learn," the tutor told himself as he resolutely ignored the tired, red-eyed glances in his direction. "He's been allowed too much freedom, and he has to grow up sooner or later. I prefer that it happen now. Better for him to suffer in my hands than in his father's."

All the same, however, he continued to fail in his efforts, the barrier separating him and Aubin proving to be much more formidable than he'd first expected. And when his thoughts flew back to the ongoing stories Aubin shared at the supper-table—of his adventures in some strange, foreign land choked with the most fantastical elements and especially of the odd fondness that suffused every reference he made of Aelfric—his confusion deepened as did his sympathy (the latter point surprising him, even).

He turned the matter over and over in his mind and presently emerged with the conclusion that Aubin was in danger of suffering a breakdown of some kind, no thanks to the painful isolation into which his father thought fit to force him. His poetic flights, his daily wanderings into the wood, his current obsession with life beyond the realm of logic and practicality—all pointed in the direction of a boy who was hopelessly lonely and in such desperate need of companionship, that he'd even managed to conjure up a friend by the name of Aelfric, who'd lead him off into these strange and wonderful worlds that could only be found in a rich, imaginative mind as Aubin's.

After a few days of thwarted purpose, LaCaille decided to follow his pupil after his lessons, stalking Aubin as he lost himself in the misty wood. He needed to take on a more scientific approach to this problem, he'd told himself, and the first thing he ought to do was to observe the boy at a discreet distance, to note down every detail of the latter's behavior, and to catalogue them later in his room for a more thorough exploration. Perhaps a few formulas might prove to be helpful in determining the solution to this dilemma.

Aubin wasn't difficult to shadow. He took familiar paths though LaCaille was surprised at discovering he didn't interact with his environment the way he did before. He simply walked forward with hasty and eager steps, his figure once again taking on that strange, fairy-like air as he moved deeper into the wood, the faint shimmer of his hair and skin beckoning to his tutor with the same hypnotic intensity as it did previously. And as before, LaCaille began to feel as though he were encroaching on territory to which he didn't belong—one far contrary to his world of tidy taxonomies and clear-cut systems and methodologies. It was a world where every stone had its own voice, every blade of grass had its own song to sing; every crumbling piece of bark had its own spell to cast.

He presently found himself at the edge of a small glade, in the middle of which was a pond half-choked with bright, violet irises. He stared in amazement at the profusion of these flowers in such a small patch of land. But it was in even greater amazement that he watched Aubin stretch himself down on his stomach at the edge of the pond, staring intently at the water as though searching for something. And when it seemed as though he'd waited too long, Aubin sat up and edged closer to the water, carefully picking out one of the water-irises, which he touched with a lover's fondness, grazing his fingers over the brilliant petals before bending down to kiss it. He pulled away and murmured something to the flower, and a wave of mild jealousy swept over LaCaille as he watched.

There was something in this all-too-private moment he'd just violated with his spying that touched a certain nerve in him—one he'd never before even considered. And he wondered at it.

Perhaps it was the fact that Aubin, even in his delusion, was able to discover something of which LaCaille was wholly ignorant. Perhaps it was the vibrant joy in the boy's features brought on by the kiss. Perhaps it was the unjaded air of a young, neophyte lover. The scholar could barely hazard a guess. All he knew at that moment was how bereft he suddenly felt, how denied he was of a certain something of which Aubin obviously had in abundance.

Aubin presently yawned, stretched languorously, and then curled up at the edge of the pond, falling asleep in an instant.

"Utter nonsense!" LaCaille ground out as he forced himself away from the tree behind which he crouched. "This is idiocy! What can be gained with all these ridiculous notions of—what—love? Enchantment? Bah! Storybook trifles meant for thoughtless children!"

He had half a mind to march up to his pupil, wake him roughly, and order him back to the cottage, but he kept himself in check. Aubin, he was forced to concede, deserved this moment, regardless of the tutor's opinions on the matter. He'd convinced himself; after all, that he'd done everything he could to help him.

He stole one final glance in the direction of the sleeping boy. Then he shrugged and walked off, brooding as he went.

Midway through, he froze in his tracks, blinking. A sudden image assailed his mind—or, rather, it was finally noticed amid the jumble of thoughts crammed in his brain. It was a fleeting image of a figure emerging from the pond—a pale figure—a boy in a brilliant suit of violet and green, a thin band of gold encircling his dark head. He swam—or perhaps he walked through chest-deep water toward Aubin—LaCaille couldn't accurately recall—a faint smile on his lips, a white hand appearing from the water to touch Aubin's hair. He might have said something—or whispered something—to the sleeping figure.

The scholar held his head in his hands as he sighed heavily. This was all too much. The wood and its odd effects were beginning to make him hallucinate. He fought off the image and hurried onward, his pace turning into a jog, and the relief that washed over him the moment he first caught sight of the cottage's gabled roof was truly beyond words.

• • • •

SEVERAL MORE DAYS OF ineffectual and desperate efforts on LaCaille's part produced nothing more than the same distracted pupil, whose fascination for the wood had now deepened to an alarming level. It seemed as though the more emphasis the tutor placed on the lessons, the more Aubin slipped from his frantically grasping fingers.

Aubin's longing could easily be sensed now, his pained gaze out the window clearly speaking of a heart firmly and irrevocably fixed on something that lay far beyond the flimsy glass barrier—something that had laid claim on his very soul, though LaCaille continued to struggle against such ridiculously groundless and primitive notions. Aubin spent greater lengths of time in his room, reading, writing, painting, or at times simply deep in melancholy thought, the shadows on his normally bright features indicative of a monumental inner struggle. A choice perhaps? A decision he was forced to face? It felt like it, LaCaille thought helplessly. Even during their meals, Aubin was distracted enough to eat only a portion of his food before excusing himself and walking off to his room.

"It's this damned cottage," he ground out as he glanced furiously around him. Mercantile sparseness and severity taunted him from all corners, and he himself began to feel his own scientific powers wane. "There's something about this feeble, crumbling pile of wood and thatch that drains one's life dry. I'm certain if I were to spend much more time in this vile house, I'd be reduced to a dribbling imbecile, the same way Aubin is now being reduced to an insensible shadow of himself."

If he weren't so angry, LaCaille would have easily caught the odd, superstitious nature of his words, and he would have infuriated himself even more. As it were, however, he remained in some confusion at the near-desperate circumstances in which he now found Aubin as well as himself. Their lessons lost their structure till the tutor was fumbling his way through the fog of science and art in violent juxtaposition. His evening hours were spent staring in bewildered silence at the incomprehensible jumble of scribbles that packed his journals.

Ignace Fournier arrived on schedule, and he couldn't have chosen a worse time for his visit. And strange though it might seem at first, the cottage had taken on a life of its own in his presence—as though the man's very essence was quickly and readily absorbed by every wall and every ceiling and every piece of furniture, and this essence was reflected back in the sudden deadening of one's senses and mental faculties. The air was stifling and heavy in spite of LaCaille's efforts at airing out the cottage by flinging the windows wide open. The philosophy of wealth, power, and consumer exchange loomed as a cloaked shadow over them. The principles of balance and surpluses, the baser sources of monetary and property acquisition, foreign and altogether terrifying forces were now stirring in their ashen piles, commanded to rise and breathe in the merchant's presence.

"Where's the boy?" Fournier thundered even before he'd shed his traveling-clothes, and a pale, sickly-looking Aubin was brought to him. "Leave me with my son for now, Monsieur, and be assured you'll have your turn."

The slamming of the study door silenced LaCaille's protests, and LaCaille forced himself to walk away—as far away as he could manage from that room, where he knew the worst was about to happen.

He walked out into the wood, burdened with a thought that had crept stealthily into his mind the minute he espied his employer's coach before the front door. It was an absurd thought, he was quick to judge, but it was tenacious in its hold, and it continued to haunt him in spite of all his efforts at fending it off. Familiar ideas, theories, formulas, and systems seemed to have lost their talismanic effect; he tried to divert his attention with them, but his heart remained painfully weighted, and nothing but the fogged image of a despondent Aubin filled his mind's eye. The faint voice at the back of his mind had gathered its strength. With the boy's image lingering, came quiet and insistent reminders of LaCaille's humanity, till he wandered blindly through familiar misty paths in utter confusion over his own purpose.

"I must return," he said instead and turned around.

Parental justice was sure and swift—at least in that household. Ignace Fournier was in the sitting room, nursing injured pride with liquor. The cane that had long been relegated to the darkest corner of the study leaned against the man's armchair, ominous even in its stylishly simple craftsmanship. He regarded LaCaille in black silence for a moment before speaking, turning his gaze back to the fire that blazed brightly in the hearth.

"Your pay, Monsieur, will be withheld until I see results in my son. Tomorrow morning, exactly an hour before your usual school time, I expect both of you back in the study—and I expect to see you make liberal use of this cane as you've been instructed before. And if I see resistance—if I hear a word of equivocation or protest—by God, I'll thrash you and the boy, myself, till the cane breaks."

"If I may speak, Monsieur," LaCaille began.

"No, you may not speak. I hired you for a purpose, and a month's time has brought me worse results than I'd expected. You've no excuse—only a second chance at proving yourself worth the money I'm willing to surrender."

"You expect a miracle where it can never happen."

"I expect, M. LaCaille, a reasonable exchange of money and services, and that's all. Good night to you."

LaCaille abruptly turned around and hurried to the study, where he found his pupil kneeling on the floor by his school chair, bracing himself weakly as he struggled to stand up. It proved to be difficult with his trousers gathered at his knees and shackling his legs. LaCaille helped him to his feet, feeling the shivering figure as Aubin leaned heavily against him while he reached down to pull his trousers up with trembling hands. Nothing was said between tutor and student for some time as LaCaille helped the boy fasten his clothes back up, the dreadful silence between them broken only by the lad's stifled sniffling.

"Come. I'll help you back to your room," LaCaille said as he guided Aubin out.

The walk upstairs was long and laborious; LaCaille shuddered as he wondered about the amount of force used on the boy, for Aubin seemed almost crippled from his father's caning. The following morning would prove to be yet another catastrophe, he thought, given Aubin's physical condition. How his employer would miss understanding the possibility of cruel physical punishment effecting completely opposite results in Aubin, he couldn't imagine.

"Resistance shares an equal chance with surrender," he muttered with a shake of his head. "And with this boy's temperament, I wouldn't be surprised to see him attempt to fight against his father's tyranny."

LaCaille sat by Aubin's bedside that evening, watching his pupil struggle for sleep as he lay on his stomach, periodically breaking the stillness with a restless and painful shifting under the covers as he sought a more comfortable position. His thoughts were swirling with many ideas and many revelations he'd never before considered, let alone believed. As it were, however, he was thrust into a situation far, far removed from the comfortable organization and systematic analysis of all things physical.

"As is Aubin," he whispered, understanding finally dawning on him. "And his father."

He turned the thought over and over in his mind with all the care and thoroughness of a natural philosopher. There were three worlds in the cottage, he told himself. All were crammed tightly under one roof, each jostling violently against the other for a legitimate place, but in the end, only one could prevail. The structure, after all, was created by one force and continued its existence under that power—with all the antiquated volumes on economics, the endless collections of accounting journals, the rigidly organized accoutrements used in the recording of monetary flow day in an day out, year after year. That cottage was Ignace Fournier's mercantile world, and it didn't have room for LaCaille's scientific intellectualism, nor did it offer refuge for Aubin's artistic beauty. For all three to live together under one roof spelled nothing but disaster, and LaCaille knew Aubin would be the weakest force, given his age and his yet improperly channeled tendencies. Aubin would be the first to be crushed under commerce's relentless weight.

LaCaille's gaze dropped to his feet. He'd say this was all rubbish, but he couldn't, and he wondered if he were going mad.

• • • •

THE POND GAVE OFF AN unearthly glow in the darkness. The water-irises looked even livelier then when seen in the day. LaCaille couldn't understand the reasons behind this odd visual phenomenon, but he now realized moments existed when even science failed to offer clear answers to certain questions.

"Well," he sighed resignedly as he turned his attention back to his thickly wrapped burden. "Then again, I'm now in his world, and I'm forced within my limits of understanding."

Beside him stood a feverish and injured Aubin, whom he'd covered with a blanket with which to stave off the midnight chill. The boy teetered on his feet as he struggled to stay awake and upright. His exhaustion was too great, as were his emotional scarring and physical pain. It was all he could do to lean bonelessly against his tutor as they both stood at the edge of the pond.

LaCaille shook his head as he stared back at the glistening water, still unable to believe what he was doing. He cleared his throat after a great deal of hesitation, and he quietly called out for someone whom he never thought existed, begging for assistance from forces he'd long dismissed as inconsequential superstitions. He felt mortified at the mere thought of his going through this, but something in him spurred him on with wordless reassurances.

"Aelfric," he said again and again, pausing each time and waiting with his breath held. "Aelfric, please come."

And so for several moments he pled for help despite his embarrassment and waited uncomfortably for something to answer his calls.

Something did, eventually, though the wait felt like an excruciating eternity.

A familiar figure emerged from the water's depths—even in the darkness, LaCaille recognized the vivid costume, the thin band of gold encircling a head of dark hair and pale skin, the bright, bright eyes that echoed the richness of the water-irises' petals. The boy in the water stared questioningly at LaCaille for a second, and science and enchantment came together and fell into step.

LaCaille brought Aubin forward and gently helped him into the pond. He watched the bundled figure regain some strength at the feel of water enveloping him, and Aubin released his hold on his tutor, moving forward on his own till he reached Aelfric's side.

What a curious sight, LaCaille noted as he watched the pair meet. What a fascinating picture they made, half-submerged in the water, surrounded by clusters of water-irises and countless points of light that broke the fathomless depths of the pond. None of it made sense to him. None. But he was fascinated still, and he even smiled in answer to the one of gratitude expressed by Aelfric.

"Take care of him. He needs you desperately," LaCaille said with a nod, which Aelfric returned with more grace and dignity as he wrapped an arm around Aubin's shoulder, holding the boy close. Ah, the tutor thought with some amusement. This enchanted creature must be a prince—at least most definitely a nobleman.

The two boys slowly sank under the water, with Aelfric holding LaCaille's gaze though Aubin seemed to be struggling with sleep still as he leaned his head against his companion's shoulder. LaCaille followed their descent till nothing was left but a small, gentle ripple where they once stood, and though he wished to gaze down on the water in hopes of catching a rare glimpse of the remarkable world that now welcomed his pupil, he held himself back and contented himself with regarding the water-irises as they continued to gather all the strange secrets of that misty wood.

He sighed once he was assured of his solitude, and he turned around and made his way back to the cottage. He realized he was going to be leaving in the morning—most assuredly thrown out by an irate father who'd be discovering his son's ungrateful, undutiful rebellion. Ignace Fournier would never know the truth, of course. Till the end of his life, he'd believe young Aubin had simply run away in defiance of his parent's wishes.

LaCaille was pleased with the thought—even more so with the notion that for one oddly glorious, fleeting moment, he'd actually touched magic.

"Oh, heavens," he said, glancing up at the midnight sky as he neared the cottage. "I really must be going mad." Then he laughed quietly, shaking his head, his mind clearing itself by randomly touching on a very problematic chemical formula with which he'd long been struggling.

# Don't miss out!

Visit the website below and you can sign up to receive emails whenever Hayden Thorne publishes a new book. There's no charge and no obligation.

https://books2read.com/r/B-A-LFQC-OVCBB

**BOOKS 2 READ**

Connecting independent readers to independent writers.

# About the Author

I've lived most of my life in the San Francisco Bay Area though I wasn't born there (or, indeed, the USA). I'm married with no kids and three cats.

I started off as a writer of gay young adult fiction, specializing in contemporary fantasy, historical fantasy, and historical genres. My books ranged from a superhero fantasy series to reworked and original folktales to Victorian ghost fiction.

I've since expanded to gay New Adult fiction, which reflects similar themes as my YA books and varies considerably in terms of romantic and sexual content.

While I've published with a small press in the past, I now self-publish my books. Please visit my site for exclusive sales and publishing updates.

Read more at https://haydenthorne.com.